Meatball Taster Publishing, LLC

These Men

Cathy,

Enjoy the
menage!

Andrea Smith

Andrea Smith
4/1/2014

These Men

By Andrea Smith

ISBN-13: 978-1-497-44880-3 (Paperback)

ISBN13: 978-0-578-12259-5 (E-Book)

Meatball Taster Publishing, LLC

Acknowledgements

Thank you to my Facebook Street Team - each and every one of you for your continued support and reminders that yes, I could write this story, because time and time again, I had my doubts!

To Ashlee Porte, who I can always count on to tell me like it is - Ma loves ya!

To my comrades in The Erotica Consortium: C.D. Reiss, Shay Savage, K. Bromberg, JA Huss, KI Lynn, Ella James, and Alessandra Torre - you ladies are awesome and I totally love what you write! It was an honor and a pleasure to have my novella introduced as part of "Bend."

And a special shout-out to Author Kennedy Kelly, Janett Gomez, Nicole Duke and Kandace Milostan for beta feedback! You ladies rock!

Cover Design: Louisa Maggio @ L.M. Creations

Editing: Janell Parque

Formatting: Tami Norman

Playlist for "These Men"

"I'll Stand By You"	The Pretenders
"Something To Talk About"	Bonnie Raitt
"My Prerogative"	Bobby Brown
"Sexual Thing"	Poison
"Who Says You Can't Go Home"	Bon Jovi
"Waiting on the World to Change"	John Mayer
"Dreams"	The Cranberries
"We Belong"	Pat Benatar
"Losing My Religion"	R.E.M.
"I Want Your Sex"	George Michaels
"Money for Nothing"	Dire Straits

Table of Contents

I'd been on the road for three days and, to be honest, I was tired of seeing green and white signs along the side of the road, charting my progress, or lack thereof, as the case might be, and staying in flea bag motels because of my strained budget. Traveling across the country sounded awesome until around the end of day two. Now, it was simply a matter of my being impatient to reach my destination.

Here I was, Paige Elizabeth Matthews, 22 years-old, leaving my parents' home in Napa, California to carve out a career and an appropriate life for myself—that was how my father had put it to me. In other words, I was being shoved from the nest for my own good.

It wasn't as if I hadn't been raised or educated properly, because I had. I'd graduated in January from Cal State with a degree that was of little use to me in Napa, but which would serve me well with some government agency such as say, the FBI? Yep, according to my father, that would be a perfect fit for me and my degree.

Yeah, I knew he'd been on the phone several times with my older brother, Trace, who was moving his way up the bureau ladder in D.C. I had relented and filled out the application for an administrative internship at my parents' urging. I assumed my brother had pulled the appropriate strings to get me selected for the program.

Sweet.

I was okay with it; I mean there was nothing to keep me in Napa. No love connections, no attachments with close friends. I'd never been much of the girly-girl who had a flock of BFFs that I shared everything with while we shopped or had our nails done.

In that respect, I was kind of a loner. Truth be told, I related much better with the male species than the female. It was probably because I'd been raised around vineyards, and the fact that vineyards employed a lot of guys made it just that much more convenient. And, to be honest? I enjoyed the attention of men. Actually, *craved* the attention of men might be more accurate.

Maybe too much.

I knew that was yet another reason my parents were kind of eager to send me off. They weren't always comfortable with my "appreciation" of the opposite sex. The fact that I had been dating several different guys simultaneously had seemed to cause them a fair amount of angst over the last several months, especially when they had gotten their names mixed up time and time again.

They would go on and on about how proud they were that my oldest brother, Easton - who I barely knew - had settled down in the U.S. with his new wife, Darcy, and their baby boy, Weston.

From there, the conversation moved onto Trace, and about how he too, had settled down…and how much they loved his wife, Lindsey, and how proud they were of their beautiful grand-babies Harper and Jackson.

They wanted the same for me—that was obvious. I just wasn't really sure if I wanted that; I couldn't picture myself living that kind of a life—at least not for a very long time. I hadn't really had any serious relationships and my instinct told me that was because I hadn't found my demographic yet—if that makes any sense at all.

I pulled off at the next exit to fill my gas tank and give Trace a quick call on my cell, to let him know that I'd be reaching their place in another few hours.

I pulled my jacket tighter around me as I fumbled with the gas cap and got the pump going. It was damp and chilly; the remnants of winter were still in the air for the first of March in eastern Pennsylvania.

He answered his cell, recognizing my number. "Where are you?" he asked, as if he were worried.

"Somewhere in Pennsylvania," I answered, chewing on a nail. "I should be at your place before dark."

"Okay, Paige, we'll be here. Drive carefully, you hear?"

"Yes, Trace," I sighed, rolling my eyes. He could be caring I suppose, but I also knew he was doing this more for Mom and Dad than for me. We just were too far apart in age to be that close.

"We're looking forward to having you stay with us," he lied, "Lindsey's got your room waiting for you. I think you're really going to like the internship, Paige. I think it just might be what you need."

I sighed. "Thanks for letting me stay with you guys. I'll try to stay out of your way, I promise."

Silence.

"See you soon," he said.

Chapter 1

I fumbled with the lock on the front door, trying to shift the bags of groceries I had in my arms to one side in order to turn the knob. I was kind of worn out and it was just past noon.

My lovely sister-in-law, Lindsey, had left me with a full shopping/errand list this morning, rousing my ass out of bed at seven-thirty. On a *Saturday* no less.

I'd been up fairly late, getting a lecture from big brother Trace, right before he left on some covert FBI mission. His lecture was all about earning my keep around here, acting responsibly, setting a better example for the babies. He felt that I could be a bigger help to Lindsey, when she had clients to visit with the little decorating business she and her mother Samantha had going, yadda, yadda, yadda.

"Paige," Trace had said, his voice carrying that serious, authoritative and slightly-*tyrannical* tone that he almost never used with Lindsey. "Lindsey and I talked about you doing a little more pitching in around here. It's not like you pay rent or anything, so how's about taking on some responsibilities and maybe curtailing some of the partying?"

"I don't mind helping out," I shrugged, "but what's the deal with my partying?" I questioned, eying my older brother warily.

"Hey, what you do and who you do it with is your business—don't get me wrong. I know you're only twenty-two and just now getting out from under Mom and Dad's roof, but we've got kids here—babies, and well…"

He was obviously uncomfortable with the subject matter, so I took the opportunity to interrupt. "Look, Trace, if it's a problem that I brought a couple of guys here for the night, I just won't do it anymore. But Christ, it's not like Harper and Jackson are old enough to know what's going on. I mean, *seriously?*"

"It's not just the fact that you brought a couple of random dudes home over the past few weeks, it's that you've shown a total disregard for the rest of us, you know?"

"No, I'm not following you, big brother," I semi-snapped. "It's not as if I fucked them on the spotless floor of your family room, while you and Lindsey were watching 'Criminal Minds.'"

His green eyes blazed an ultra shade of pissed.

"You're loud and disruptive when you…*entertain*, Paige. It makes Lindsey uncomfortable, and uh…me too. Lindsey and I would prefer that you not do that anymore. It'd be better if you stay over at your boyfriend's places in the future."

"Boyfriends?" I snorted with a laugh. "They weren't *boyfriends*, they were hook-ups. And are you seriously gonna sit there and act like you never had casual sex? That every chick you've ever laid was a *girlfriend?* Because if you say yes, then I'm calling you out on it."

I started to get up to leave the room, but Trace wasn't finished with the lecture just yet.

"Hold up, Paige. Look, I'm not one to lecture you on the moral fine points of 'hooking up' or having fuck buddies. And for the record, my sexual history is none of your goddamn business, and it's not part of this conversation, because I'm not gonna preach like that. What I *am* gonna tell you is that this is *our* home and you *will* respect the ground rules, or you'll have to move out. Got it?"

Fuck, he's pissed.

I shrugged, clasping my hands together. "Sure. I apologize, Trace. It won't happen again."

Right then and there I knew that my living arrangement wasn't going to work. Somewhere along the way, Trace had been domesticated.

Huh, who'd have thought?

It wasn't like I'd seen him a lot over the past say, twelve or thirteen years, but Holy Mother of Christ, I could see that my good ol' big brother was indeed pussy-whipped. Certainly not the same guy that left Napa all of those years ago with a bevy of blondes mourning his departure.

My other older brother, Easton, was even more of a stranger to me than Trace. Probably because he hadn't been born to my mother. I had only brief, scattered memories of him growing up. He would stay with us during the summers back then. I had been in pigtails and braces at the time, but I had seen more of him over the past few weeks since I'd been here, than over the twenty-two years that I'd been on this planet.

His wife, Darcy, seemed like a pretty cool chick. She and Lindsey were tight, both being the same age and having been friends before they became sisters-in-law, but for whatever reason, I could relate to Darcy more than I could to Lindsey.

Yeah, they were like a little over a year older than me, but with having kids and all that, I guess it put them in a different maturity category; though, if I were a betting person, I'd say that Darcy had done her share of dudes, more so than Lindsey for sure.

I filed that away for future reference. If Trace and Lindsey were going to be so fucking uptight, maybe Easton and Darcy would open their huge house to little sister. I doubted that my craving for…*male attention* would be as off-putting over there as it apparently was over here.

Pfft!! Was Lindsey up-tight or what?

I was overjoyed that she'd taken the rug rats with her today. I don't think I could've accomplished everything she had put on my 'to-do' list while having to drag those two along with me. Harper was at least somewhat manageable at two and a half, but Jackson was another fucking story. I mean, I don't do diapers.

At all.

I knew that someday I would, because having a little rug rat of my own was in the plan—eventually. But that was a long ways off.

I'd been at Trace and Lindsey's for about six weeks now. I had started going through my P.T. at Quantico a few weeks ago. (P.T. means Physical Training for those of you not familiar with military lingo.) And let me add that physical training is a bitch under any circumstances, but for someone who hadn't bothered to condition before starting the program (like me) it was damn near suicide.

I gathered up the groceries, taking them into the kitchen and setting them on the countertop.

Fuck!

Lindsey had added yet *another* one of her pink post-it notes to the fridge.

What now?

She must've stopped home while I was out.

(Beotch.)

Paige - Forgot to tell you that I have a plumber stopping by this afternoon between one and two. He's to fix the shower in the master bath and leave the bill with you. - L

Okay, whatevs.

At least I didn't have to go back out. Trying to navigate around the metropolitan D.C. area *was* a bitch. Hell, I don't know how many times I ended up in Maryland instead of freakin' Virginia!

I had just finished putting the groceries away when there was a knock on the door. I opened it to a dark-haired, brown-eyed dude that had a fucking tool belt on.

Damned if he wasn't built, too.

"Hey," he said, and I noticed right off that his voice was deep and sexy. "I'm scheduled to check out a leaking shower faucet in the master bath. Are you Mrs. Matthews?"

"Hi," I said, flashing him a smile as I opened the door wider to let him in. "Actually, I'm the sister-in-law from hell," I joked. "But Lindsey did leave a note saying you'd be here. Come on in."

Now it was his turn to flash a smile at me, showing perfectly even white teeth. The name embroidered on his blue work shirt read "Jason."

"Well, Jason," I said, with just a hint of flirtation, "Let me show you the way."

Fuck, his hair was thick and curly. His arms and shoulders were muscular; belly flat. I was guessing he was late twenties, possibly thirty.

Did I mention he was wearing a tool belt?

Yep—definitely loved the tool belt, especially the way that it was slung low on his hips. It even made a sexy jingling sound when he walked.

He followed me upstairs and then down the hallway towards the master suite. I gestured my arm towards the bathroom door that was just off of their bedroom.

I couldn't help but notice his sexy swagger as he walked past me into the bathroom, bending over just a bit to place his toolbox on the tiled floor. This guy exuded sexual energy from every fucking pore. Trust me, that's something I pick up on within seconds of meeting someone.

"I'll just leave you to it," I called out, going back downstairs. "I'll be in the kitchen if you have any questions."

"Yep," he called back, already starting to assess the plumbing situation in the bathroom.

He returned downstairs no more than ten minutes later, wiping his hands on a rag. "Just needed a washer replaced and I had one in my toolbox. I went ahead and checked the fitting and it was fine, so I went ahead and re-greased it. Tested the shower head out and it's working fine. No more dripping."

"That *was* fast," I said throwing a bit of a double entendre into the remark. "I guess that's a good thing *sometimes*, huh?"

He gave me a good-natured laugh, his eyes glancing down to my legs in a subtle, but obviously not too-subtle way. I bit back a girlish grin as I watched him swiftly pull out the bill slip from his back pocket and jot some numbers down on it. Ripping the top copy from the pad, I caught the sexy-ass grin he tossed my way as he handed it to me.

Oh yeah. Game friggin' *on*.

And before you go and get all judgy on me? I'm a woman who has an affinity for hotties with a Y-chromosome.

Sue me.

And I could tell that this guy wasn't interested in anything serious.

The good news? Neither was I.

"You're good to go," he said with his grin still in place, wiping his brow with the back of his hand.

"Replacing that washer must've given you quite a workout, huh?" I asked him, feigning innocence.

He looked back over at me, the smile stretching even further across his face. "Why do you ask?"

"Well, you just look like you could use some ice-cold water," I shrugged. "That's all."

"I'll take some water," he replied quietly, leaning up against the counter.

I broke the minor eye-fucking thing we had going there for a second, and made my way over to the cupboard and grabbed a glass. After it was filled, I hopped up on the same counter top that he was still leaning against and handed it over.

Jason's eyes made their way down my tanned legs again as he raised the icy glass up to his full lips, drinking the offered beverage.

I rubbed my palms over my thighs for bonus points, masquerading it as a nervous gesture.

He replied with a loud swallow, breaking the glass-and-lips contact to give me an almost sheepish look.

"No worries, I'm a loud swallower too."

That's when he nearly dropped the glass. And before our flirtatious dialogue turned into something from a porn video, I decided it was time for a little action.

Hopping off of the counter, I made the entire two foot distance between us and took the glass of water out of his hand. Keeping eye contact with him the entire time, I took a long swallow from it.

I think *this* is what I loved about everything sexual: the control of it.

The power.

I thought of myself as someone who was comfy with my overall sexuality, and I also loved to tease a little bit. But with the way good ol' Jason was looking at me now, he was ready to move past the teasing stage.

He stood up to his full height, his chest brushing the backs of my fingers as they maintained their hold on the glass. My eyes widened a bit as I watched him lean in, thinking that he was going for the kiss. I promptly closed them, and waited.

But his lips never did touch mine.

My eyes were still shut when I felt a hard suck on the side of my neck. Gasping and reacting, I took a step back and found my back up against Lindsey's granite counter. Jason's arms were now on either side of me, trapping me and turning me the hell on.

His mouth was now apologizing, as his tongue soothed the now-tender spot that was just below my ear. He then made his way to the underside of my jaw, nipping and licking.

I arched my neck to give him easier access, but apparently he was done with my neck, for now, because his hand reached back and very softly gripped my hair and tilted my head back down to eye-level.

Licking my bottom lip when he leaned back in, I fully expected an actual kiss this time. And still, he didn't deliver. Instead, he kissed the corner of my lips.

I *seriously* loved the way his stubble felt on my skin, I'd decided. That was when I tried to take the moment into my own hands and went in for the kill.

I was almost to his mouth when his hand fisted even tighter in my hair, preventing me from closing the mere centimeters I had left. He pulled back, letting go of my hair, and looked at me with raised eyebrows and a confident smirk.

"Is *this* what you had in mind?" he asked.

I matched his smirk with one of my own and upped the wattage. "Well actually, what I had in mind was some lip-to-lip action. Know what I mean? So, if you don't mind…"

"Well, had I known *that*," he confessed mischievously, "I would have brought my tip jar."

That's when we both cracked up, letting the humor of it all wash over us. Finally, when we both managed to collect our wits again, I sighed. Clearly, the moment of sexual tension had come to a close and it was my cue to send this guy on his merry little way.

I turned away from him and fished out a pen from one of the drawers and signed my name at the bottom of the forgotten bill. Handing the slip back to him, Jason met my gaze with a heated one of his own.

"So, I'm officially off the clock, eh?" he asked.

I felt my eyebrows nearly reach my hairline. "Umm...yeah?"

"That's good."

Yeah, I wasn't following. Until I watched his eyes travel to the button of my denim cut-offs and back up to my face, regarding me with a look that was asking me a question.

"Lip-to-lip action, you said?" The mischief was back. "May I?"

Sweet baby Jesus. Does he mean...what I think he means?

He took a very unrushed step towards me. And there was pretty much *nothing* I was going to do in that moment to dissuade him. His fingers brushed up my thighs when he was back in kissing distance, making their way to the top of my shorts and skimming over the skin that was just right above it.

With one hand, he unfastened the button and tilted his head over to my ear and gave the lobe a quick nip. I felt my chest rise and rapidly fall as he pushed the denim down my legs.

I watched him kneel to the floor only to look back up at me, "You didn't answer me," he said.

"Yes." I quickly replied.

He smiled briefly, and brought his face to my panty-covered pussy. I felt something wet and warm pushing against it from the other side of the material, and my head fell back as my arms braced my body on either side of the counter.

Using his hands to spread my legs a little wider, he began to suck hard on the damp fabric. I moaned when I felt his tongue push as far as it could go, only to retreat back into his mouth in exchange for a set of fingers. The fingernails of his other hand grazed my lower tummy as his talented fingers continued to lightly strum my slit.

"Tease," I called him, not even knowing whether or not he heard me, being that it was quickly followed by another frustrated moan.

But he must have heard me, because those fingers rubbed a little harder, and I felt the tip of his tongue on my clit through my panties right before he asked, "Do you want me to stop?"

I looked down at him, and he chuckled softly as he took that specific moment to pull my underwear all the way down. Leaving them to pool at my feet, he didn't waste any time at all before his tongue sank *all* the way into my wetness.

"*Shit*," I whispered to no one in particular.

He pulled back only to take an entire lip into his mouth, nursing on it softly. Jason did the same thing with the other one before French-kissing my pussy for a second time.

My knuckles were completely bleached, as my hands clung to the counter, because I was pretty sure they were the only things holding me up at this point. The only sounds in the room were my hardening intakes of air and the wet noises of his mouth eating me.

My hips were now beginning to grind up against his jaw. I felt his hands cover mine on the edge of the counter, making sure I didn't lose my grip.

He tongued my clit, and I was *so fucking close*.

"You have one minute to come," he told me, licking up my entire slit.

I managed an airless laugh and whimpered as two thick fingers entered me, "Or...?"

"Or I *make* you come," he replied quietly.

I loved being under pressure to come. There's just something about having constraints like that put into place that makes that pre-O sensation draw out even longer, which in effect, makes the orgasm blow that much harder when it is released.

This was one of those times.

I closed my eyes, my head tilted up towards the ceiling, and I let myself totally submerge into this pool of pleasure that Jason had created for me with his very talented tongue and his probing, thick fingers, which were giving my sweet spot the 'ol come-hither motion at that very moment.

I felt my core turn to liquid as I melted into the magical thrumming of his tongue and fingers in unison, on both my clit and my sweet spot, ready to give him exactly what he'd ordered just moments before. I moaned loudly, my hips starting to thrust upward to lessen his journey.

"What the hell?" I heard someone shriek…from somewhere.

Immediately, Jason's warmth left me. My eyes simultaneously flew open, the hazy fog of being 'almost there' quickly dissipated as I saw Lindsey's horrified face standing about six or seven feet away, aghast at what she had just viewed.

She had clamped her only free hand over Harper's eyes, her other arm cradled a still-sleeping Jackson against her chest.

"Get out," she hissed, and to be honest, I wasn't sure if she meant Jason, or me, or quite possibly the both of us.

Jason hurriedly stood up, grabbed his tool box and got the hell out as quickly as any man could, his erection still very evident underneath his navy blue work pants.

I slid from the countertop, bending over to pick up my panties and shrug them back on. Lindsey was still glaring at me, evidently too fucking pissed to have the good manners to give me some privacy. Harper was squirming around, trying to move Lindsey's hand away from where it still covered her eyes, but she couldn't budge it.

"Timing," I said, pulling my cutoffs up and fastening the button, "is fucking everything," I finished, brushing past her and going to my room.

Chapter 2

It was my sixth week of physical training, but it felt as if it had been years instead of weeks. I stood in the weight room, at five-fifteen in the morning—that's right—five-fucking-fifteen, watching myself in the mirrored wall of the room, doing curls with free weights clutched in both hands.

Fuck, why in the hell did I get assigned this time frame for a personal work-out?

It was punishment, pure and simple. But it *was* required, and since I'd done a good job of pissing off my instructor, it was what it was.

I glanced around the large, carpeted room. There were only three other people in here, all guys. The thing was, I had to clock in and out, so it wasn't as if I could ditch it without getting busted, and then I'd be in more trouble, if that were even possible.

Neither Trace nor Lindsey were speaking to me and hadn't been for three weeks. I was, as they say, *persona non grata* at the Trace Matthews residence.

Kicking me out was totally their prerogative, I got that. But why the fuck had I been forced to endure yet *another* one of Trace's lectures?

He had even asserted that I had no fucking business being in the bureau, and that I had my head stuck so far up my ass, even he couldn't pry it out. That was, if he had a mind to, which he said he clearly didn't.

Oh. What. *Ever*

I looked at my reflection. As bad as Trace had made me sound, I didn't think that I really resembled the type of loser that he'd accused me of being.

Hell, I was in the best shape that I'd ever been in physically.

My arms and legs were toned nicely; my belly firm and flat. I was taller than Lindsey; *that* had to count for something, right?

My light brown hair was long and shiny; and my dark brown eyes resembled pools of liquid chocolate, or so some dude had once told me right after we'd shared sex and a blunt.

I wiped some perspiration from my neck with my towel, placed the free weights back into the slots in the rack, and grabbed the next heavier set of weights.

I planted my legs a bit apart just as Darin, my assigned trainer, had instructed. I started once again with the curls, making sure to inhale and exhale the way that he had recommended. It really did work. I used the oxygen to my benefit, just like he said that I should.

Okay, so things at Easton's and Darcy's weren't as bad as they had been at Trace and Lindsey's, but shit, I knew that Lindsey had filled Darcy's head with pre-conceived notions about me.

The good thing was that Darcy didn't give me pink post-it notes with daily chores scribbled on them. She at least had a housekeeper and gardener at her disposal, so that took me off the hook.

Still, it seemed that Darcy didn't want to hang out much, or really converse a lot. Easton was always traveling, but hell, at least I wasn't constantly being lectured.

I was getting an income from my internship, although it was nothing to brag about for sure. Trust me, I wanted nothing more than to be on my own and not accountable to anyone else, but that just wasn't going to happen any time soon. I had to bide my time and save money along the way.

I glanced up at the clock. It was nearly five-thirty. At six I officially had to clock out, take a shower and dress for my office job at the bureau that was part of my internship training.

Once my training was complete, I would have an opportunity to apply for a permanent position with the bureau, and receive a bump in my salary. But hell, that wouldn't be for another eight months.

I commenced doing squats with the weights, just as my mentor/trainer Darin came bouncing into the weight room.

"There's my girl," he called out, flashing me a smile.

Okay. That's…different.

I'd spent a good deal of time pissing off Darin Murphy. Now for whatever reason, he acted pleased to see me. This immediately put me on alert.

Darin Murphy had been with the bureau for several years. Most recently, he'd completed an assignment in Alaska, of all places. I got the feeling that he hadn't much cared for it. Now his assignment was to torture and humiliate interns, although he liked to refer to it as "coaching." Though whenever he made said referral, I would always make sure to refer to him as *"asscrown"* in my head. And smile.

He was a hottie for sure, complete with an Irish temper that, unfortunately, I had been on the receiving end of more than once. He called me a 'slacker' amongst other things, and in all honesty, he was right.

"Cadet Matthews," he said, coming up closer, eyeballing me to make sure that I was in the correct position and really challenging my muscles. "Glad to see you made it in on time this morning. I think you were mistaken when you told me that you weren't a morning person."

He followed that with a sexy wink.

Sweet Jesus - he is flirting . . . kinda . . .

His teasing statement was because I had actually used that *lame* excuse when he had jumped my ass the previous week about clocking in late for my seven a.m. personal workouts. So, like I said, my punishment was being assigned to an earlier time slot for the next few weeks. Not only that, but it was also now on "my time," meaning I wasn't on the payroll clock like I had been when I was scheduled at seven.

I had to hang with it or get kicked out of the program, and as much as this part of it, and agents like Darin Murphy who loved to bust the chops of newbies for the pure pleasure of it, was clearly not my cup of tea, I was still determined not to fail.

Why?

Because that's what everyone expected me to do, my parents included. I sort of had a history of failure.

"Morning, sir," I addressed him, continuing my repetitions, inhaling and exhaling in timed rhythm.

"Hey, just wanted to let you know that Agent Carpenter said you're doing a good job in learning the database over in the lab. He said you're actually fairly knowledgeable with the analytical instrumentation as well. I have to admit, I'm surprised a little."

I looked over at him, quirking a brow as I finished the last repetition. "I *do* have a B.S. in Physics from Cal State," I replied, putting the free weights back into their empty slots in the rack.

"So I saw when I reviewed your file," he commented, giving me a boyish grin. "With a 3.87 G.P.A. to boot. Impressive. So, I gotta ask: why did you apply for the Visiting Scientist Program internship? Why not just apply for a job with the bureau and start making real money?"

I wiped the back of my neck with the towel. "Because I'm not twenty-three yet, Agent Murphy. I'm only twenty-two. But, by the time I finish this internship, I *will be* twenty-three. I guess I figured having the successful completion of the VSP on my resume just might bump me up a notch or three."

He cocked an eyebrow at me, and a devilish grin followed. "The operative words being 'successful' and 'completion,' Cadet Matthews," he retorted, turning and heading back. "That's totally in *your* court, babe."

And it totally was.

And I knew it.

But why did Darin Murphy care?

Chapter 3

Apparently, Memorial Day was some sort of a customary celebration in D.C. I mean, yeah, I can recall growing up and having a long weekend to mark the start of summer. I even remember going to the local Memorial Day parade, but this holiday certainly seemed to be more than that here—at least with my semi-relatives it was.

"Hey Paige," Darcy greeted as I strolled into the kitchen a little after ten a.m. to get my first cup of java. "Want to help me with some of this food? I could use someone to make the deviled eggs."

"Sure," I said, while adding a generous amount of creamer to my coffee.

I'd been up late, not getting in from Darin's until the wee hours of the morning.

Yeah, that's correct; I'd been doing my coach, which is probably not smart, but hey, there were no official rules against it at the bureau. It was simply that we had both ramped up the flirtations at work, and finally I could think of no good excuse not take Darin up on his invitation to stop by his apartment for beer and pizza one Friday night.

So far, I'd kept this quasi-relationship my own personal business, and thankfully, Darcy wasn't one to pry. But, things with Darin looked to be going from 'quasi' to 'possibly,' so having been apprised of the fact early on that Darin had been in kind of a serious relationship with my host sister-in-law, it was probably smart to clue her in.

My caffeine fix in hand, I made my way to Darcy's side and watched her torture some tomatoes as she sliced and diced. "So, why are *you* the one making the food for this barbeque, anyway? I mean, isn't that why you have Martha Stewart working for you?" I waggled my eyebrows at her.

She laughed good-naturedly. "Her last name isn't *Stewart*," she replied, "Although, I can understand how you might draw that connection."

"Yeah," I nodded, grabbing an onion that was next to the freshly-washed vegetables next to the cutting board, "Those blueberry scones she makes for the 'Lord of the Manor' are fucking awesome."

Darcy started laughing; wiping a tear from her eye that I was fairly sure was a result of the onion I was currently peeling, and not my reference to my oldest brother Easton.

"I swear Paige," she said, "You freakin' crack me up at times. I can't understand why you and Lindsey seem to rub each other the wrong way. My God, Easton is uber uptight and you seem to hold your own with him."

I was silent for a moment, contemplating what she'd obviously noticed. "It's because Easton has no expectations of me," I replied casually, peeling the next layer of skin from the onion.

"I don't understand," she said, wrinkling her forehead in confusion. "I mean I know the whole deal about him not being a blood relative and all of that, but you still consider him your brother, right?"

"Actually," I looked over at her and found that I now had her full-blown attention. "To be honest, blood or no, Easton really wasn't around all that much. And considering the age difference between Trace and me is eleven years, well there you have it. I just don't share that many memories with Easton, but I mean…it's more than that, Darcy."

"Go on," she said, scraping her diced tomatoes into a bowl of drained pasta.

"Well, they both seem like brothers to me as far as *that* goes, but Trace treats me exactly the same way that my father does—did," I corrected. "I just never seem to make the mark with either of them. Easton? Well he just says what's on his mind, good or bad, regardless of who's in the audience. I mean, I don't think he's harder—or softer—on me than anyone else."

"I get that," Darcy, replied, tossing the pasta salad. "I'm glad you realize that Easton isn't a warm and fuzzy person by nature, and not to take it personally."

"And I hear *that*," I replied, smiling. I gestured toward the onions, "Sliced or diced?"

"Hmm? Oh, diced please," she responded with a nod.

I started chopping away at the onions. "Darcy, I need to let you know something and now is probably as good of a time as any…it's kind of, well—uncomfortable."

"Go ahead," she said, watching me.

"Well, the thing is, I'm seeing someone and you actually know this person. I would've said something sooner except that I felt it was just, you know, a purely casual thing?"

She nodded, adding several dollops of mayo to her pasta salad.

"Well, the thing is, I'm thinking now that maybe it's getting to be more than just a casual thing with the two of us, and I don't want you to be uncomfortable with—"

"Say no more," she interrupted, a big grin going. "Lindsey is my best friend, but I'm here to tell you that I'm not nearly as provincial as she is. I appreciate that you haven't brought guys over—I know she and Trace had issues with it, but what the hell? This place is like a freaking zip code of its own. Easton and I have no issue with you having a steady boyfriend in your life, and having him sleep over here occasionally. So it's cool, okay?"

I looked over to where she was smiling as she tossed the rest of the seasoning into her pasta salad.

Well, that *was a piece of cake.*

"Wow, thanks," I replied. "But you need to know that the guy I'm talking about is...Darin Murphy."

I turned back to chopping my onions, wincing as I heard the glass bowl that was full of Darcy's pasta salad, hit the kitchen floor and shatter loudly.

Chapter 4

Okay, so the Memorial Day barbeque had been just a tad...*uncomfy*. Once Darcy had regained her ability to speak, she told me in no uncertain terms that it was in Darin Murphy's best interest to never step foot anywhere near their 'zip code.'

She explained that, while she no longer had feelings for him, Easton was a whole different story. She even confided to me that she suspected Easton of having had something to do with Darin getting that sudden assignment in Alaska.

"I mean, I hope he treats you better than he treated me, Paige," she told me, "But please, be *really* prepared if he doesn't." Darcy gave me a weary look.

I tossed that around in my head for a good second. "So, I guess what you're telling me is that, if I continue to see him, it needs to be kept a secret?" I asked.

She shook her head and reached over to give me the good ol' friendly arm pat. "Not at all," she said. "Just from Easton, that's all. And if you don't bring him to any family get-togethers, that'd probably be a great idea too."

The good news about the barbeque was that I was introduced to Darcy's old roommate and still close friend, Eli Chambers and his live-in partner, Cain Maddox.

God!

Those had to be two of the sexiest, drop-fucking-dead gorgeous men that I'd ever laid my chocolate-brown eyes on!

And the funny thing was, they were like night and day, literally. I mean Eli was day: boyish charm, streaky blondish/sandy locks, fair skin, blue eyes, outgoing and funnier than shit. Cain was night: quietly serious—almost brooding, raven black hair, serious brown eyes, olive complexion and somewhat reserved—until you got to know him, which for some reason, I made it a point to do.

Maybe it was because I knew that both of the dudes were gay and I didn't need to put on the whole "sex-kitten, do-me-or-die" routine. I could just be me, however bland and exhausting that was.

Yeah—exhausting.

That had been my mother's favorite adjective for me during my teen years. I guess she thought she was done having kids after having my brother Trace.

Then eleven years later?

Congratulations—it's a *girl!*

Don't get me wrong, I was never mistreated or neglected; it was more along the lines of my simply feeling invisible to them. My best guess was that's why I tended to sometimes do things for the pure shock value. I mean attention, whether positive or negative, is still attention, right?

"So how do you like D.C., Paige?" Cain asked, taking a bite out of one of the deviled eggs I'd made, and quickly dropping the remainder of it back onto his plate.

I started to reply, but he held up his hand, stifling a cough, and reached for his glass of lemonade, gulping it down. "Jesus Christ," he muttered, wiping his mouth, "How can someone fuck up deviled eggs?"

I felt myself flush, realizing my earlier suspicion had been correct.

"Sorry," I murmured sheepishly. "Actually, I think I might've sprinkled those with chili pepper instead of paprika."

"No shit," he grumbled, now starting to chuckle.

"I probably should take them back into the house and toss them," I said, starting to get up.

"Stay," he instructed mischievously, "I don't want to miss Eli's reaction when he bites into his." He nodded towards the other side of the patio, where Eli was standing next to Darcy, listening to her prattle on about something while taking the first bite of his deviled egg.

"Holy Shit!" he rasped, spitting it back out onto his plate. Everyone turned to look over at Eli, who was now taking gulps of his iced tea, and swishing it around in his mouth.

"*Fuck*, Darce," he pretty much snarled, wiping away at his mouth, "I get that everything domestic isn't your strong suit, but seriously?"

"Excuse *me?*" Darcy said, totally injured and confused.

"Shit, I can't let anyone else bite into those fire bombs," I said, giggling. "Be back in a few."

I hurried over to Darcy and Eli, explaining my faux pas with the eggs. We quickly went into 'damage control' mode, collecting the uneaten eggs off of everyone's plates, and took the platter into the house to be disposed of properly.

Once back outside, I resumed my place next to Cain. Eli had pulled up a chair and the three of us became better acquainted.

I explained to the both of them about my internship at the FBI academy, including my limited income, thus the reason I was freeloading with Easton and Darcy.

Eli shared that he worked at Baronton-Sheridan, the company owned by Darcy's father, and Easton. Cain was part-owner of a catering company in D.C. that was small, but growing steadily.

"So, how do you like living here with Easton and Darcy?" Eli asked, quirking a brow.

"You know," I replied, taking a sip of my iced tea, "They've been great, but I probably need to find a place of my own, if possible. I'm not sure what the cost of living is like here as far as rentals."

They exchanged glances.

"Honey," Eli spoke first, "I don't have a clue how much money you're making as an intern there, but I have a feeling the type of apartment you could afford would fit into one of Darcy's closets, and your roommates would be small...and furry."

"Eww," I said, wrinkling my nose. "The thing is, I have a boyfriend and well, Darcy made it plain that he isn't to stay over here, and we're not at that stage—or even *close* to being at that stage where we've discussed living together—"

"Wait a minute," Cain spoke up. "Eli and I have been tossing around the idea of getting another roommate to share expenses. We recently bought a home together in Silver Spring, and to be honest, we are a little financially strapped, what with the mortgage payment and all."

Cain looked over at Eli for input. "You'd have to pay for your own groceries, split the utilities and your rent would be $450 a month," Eli said. "And also pitch in with the housework. We don't have a staff like Darcy has," he added with a grin.

"Hmm," I replied, calculating it in my head. I still had a car payment and my pay at the bureau was really just a stipend at $1000 a month. It wouldn't leave me much to live on, but if I was frugal, I doubted I could do any better, or even as good trying to find a place of my own.

Cain could tell I was struggling to figure out whether I could manage it or not. "Babe, I gotta tell you that you can't touch an efficiency in D.C., or the surrounding area, for less than $900 a month. With us, you'll have your own room and bathroom, plus use of our fully equipped kitchen and laundry room. I mean, you don't even have any furniture, right?"

I nodded. "I've been saving up my earnings and planned on going to some second hand shops for the basics," I replied.

"So there you go," Cain continued, shrugging like it was a done deal. "And if you need a little extra money, I occasionally need help on the weekends with the catering business, so we could put you to work there, uh…as long as you promise to stay out of the deviled egg making," he finished with a wink.

I found myself grinning, not just because Cain gave me one of his sexy winks, but because my shoulders could finally relax as if an entire city had been lifted off of them. It was kind of a friggin' crazy moment because one minute, I'm living with Darcy and Easton and the next…Cain and Eli are offering to bring me in as a roomie.

Holy shit?

I glanced back over at Cain who was nodding at something Eli must have just said.

"So," I started with a huge non-resistant smile on my face, "Is this weekend too soon?"

Chapter 5

I'd been living with Cain and Eli for almost two months now, and we had settled into a pretty comfortable routine. Living with dudes was different than I expected, and with those two, it was starting to feel more like family.

It had felt a little weird for the first week or so, but after that, it felt like my home too.

I loved their brick ranch-style home that was nestled on a tree-lined street in Silver Spring. The houses weren't far apart, yet not on top of one another either. They had a fairly large backyard with a privacy fence around it, along with a deck that was right off of the kitchen that had a kick-ass hot tub/Jacuzzi combination.

We split the chores up, and took turns cooking dinner. Both Cain and Eli were great cooks and had taken me under their wings in the kitchen. I figured getting a little domestic training, compliments of my roomies, was an additional perk in our living arrangement.

Eli was just getting home from work, still dressed in his office *ensemble* as I was packing up some ingredients. And I say *ensemble*, because with Eli? That's exactly what it was. The guy dressed better than most brides do on their wedding day.

He came into the kitchen, loosening up his white tie, watching me as I put a box of angel hair pasta, tomato sauce, and fresh mushrooms in a box I planned on hauling over to Darin's. Because tonight, I was cooking for my man, and I was eager to show him my new awesome kitchen skills.

"So, I see you intend to get to your man's heart through his stomach tonight, eh?" he teased. "Don't forget the Parmesan cheese," he reminded me.

"Yeah thanks, Eli," I replied, grabbing it from the fridge. "With any luck, you won't see me for breakfast," I said with a grin.

Eli scoffed playfully. "I'm betting you two don't make it through dinner with those tight little shorts you've got going there," he remarked, picking up the stack of mail I'd placed on the kitchen table and sorting through it. "Which, by the way, you rock," he winked, giving me some of his flirtatiousness that I'd come to enjoy.

"Trust me," I replied, smiling, "I won't be offended one damn bit if he prefers me to my cooking."

"Yeah, yeah," he mumbled, shaking his head.

"I know you don't care for Darin," I remarked, grabbing the package of chicken breasts out of the sink where I had them thawing. "But so far, he's the closest thing to a steady relationship that I've had…ever. I mean, it's not just about the sex, you know?"

Eli sighed and looked up from the stack of mail.

"He's a cheater, Paige," he deadpanned. "He cheated on Darcy like it was *easy*. And I don't like the fact that you're going over there, getting all excited to play house for the night. Okay? There, I've said it." He shrugged, "Once a cheater—"

"I know, I know," I interrupted. "Always a cheater. I've heard it before."

I tossed a bag of mixed salad greens into the box and gave Eli a peck on the cheek. "I love that you're protective over me. It's something that I'm not used to, I guess," I said softly, looking up at him. "But I need to explore this relationship because it just might be right for me, okay?"

He studied me for a second, and let out a soft chuckle while shaking his head.

"Where's Maddox?" he asked, referring to Cain by his last name, which was how he always addressed him for some reason.

The fact that he had beat Cain home was pretty damn unusual, because Cain had mean ninja skills when it came to punctuality.

"Oh," he left a note on the fridge. "Playing racquetball with Steve and Lance. You're supposed to meet them at the club and make it a foursome."

"Ah shit," Eli said, looking up at the ceiling with a heavy sigh. "I'm fucking tired, and it's Friday, and that means it's chill time for me right there in front of the television. Does he not know this by now?"

I giggled at Eli's over-dramatic, sulky tone, closing up the box holding what was going to be a scrumptious meal.

"So DVR whatever it is you'd be watching, dude," I said with a shrug. "I mean, you did hear me when I said 'foursome,' right? As in four sweaty guys alone in a fiberglass-encased room with nothing to do except whack at their balls with their..." I lowered my voice to a theatrical whisper, "rackets?"

Eli gave me a playful swat as I passed him on my way out. "Brat," he growled. "Drive safely."

On my way out through the door though, I made sure to turn around with, "Oh, and try not to dent up any *hardwood* floors with your balls. I hear that's frowned upon." I gave him a stern look.

He shook his head with a hard eye-roll, closing the door with one huge-ass grin on his face.

∞∞∞∞∞∞∞∞∞∞∞∞∞∞∞∞∞∞∞∞∞∞∞∞∞∞

Eli had hit the nail on the head. Darin and I had just finished our salads when he followed me into the kitchen, where I bent over to check the Chicken Parmesan in the oven.

"Mmm," he said, coming up behind me, and rubbing my ass with the palms of both hands. I straightened up, leaning back against his strong frame.

"I can see those squats have made your glutes kind of epic there, babe," he whispered in my ear. I shivered as his lips brushed against my lobe, and then his tongue lightly flicked the outer edge.

"I'll take that as a compliment of the highest regard," I replied, "I have a very strict trainer, you see."

His arms encircled me, and I felt him nuzzle the back of my neck with his nose; he nipped gently at my skin. "How about you turn the oven down and we get a little exercise before the main course?"

I smiled against him, reaching over and turning the oven dial down to nearly nothing.

Darin lifted me up, and I immediately wrapped my bare legs around his torso, allowing him to carry me off to his king-sized bed where we enjoyed an hour of play that had very few boundaries.

We had just finished dinner, and I was loading the dishwasher, when his cell rang. He looked down at it.

"Gotta take this, babe," he said, taking several long strides out of the kitchen. I figured it was probably something with the bureau. Darin was so committed to the FBI and loved his new assignment as Intern Coordinator. He was a master of motivation; that was for damn sure.

I heard his voice raised a bit from the living room, just enough to hear him say, "I told you, Lisa, not tonight. I'm busy, babe."

Umm...?

My ears immediately went into 'eavesdrop' mode, a skill I had honed growing up, as a result of all the boundaries I had crossed with my parents. They were forever disagreeing on how to handle discipline where I was concerned. I tiptoed closer to the hallway, straining to hear his side of the conversation.

"Tomorrow then, babe. Yeah, I've got to go now. Uh huh…Okay…miss you, too."

What the hell?

I'm not much of a game player—with emotions, that is. I joined Darin in the living room right as he tossed his cell on the table.

"Who was that?" I asked point-blank.

He immediately looked over at me as if I had somehow crossed an arbitrary line with him.

"That was a friend of mine," he replied, without batting an eye. "You probably know her from the program, Lisa Benedict."

I did know her. Tall, blonde, big boobs. She was doing an internship at Quantico as well. She was another of Darin's coachees.

"So what? Are you fucking her too?" I blurted. "I mean, I couldn't help hearing part of your conversation," I said, feeling my face flush.

He looked at me directly, not masking his expression. "Hey, Paige, I mean, come on here. You and me? We're not exclusive or anything," he said, his tone clipped. "I don't nose into your business, and by the same token, I don't expect you to be nosing into mine."

I walked over to where he was standing, and made sure that my eyes met up with his.

"Huh," I raised my shoulders and let them fall. "So you're just my trainer who likes to keep it…physical. I get it. I mean, I kind of thought we had a little something going, but I'm so glad you took the time to clear *that* up."

"Hey," he replied, his hands outstretched, as if pleading his case to me. "We've *never* discussed exclusivity, and…I'm not at a place right now where I even *want* to consider it. Well, I mean, not with you at any rate, Paige. I mean, you're a knock-out and all, babe, but I don't see me getting serious with someone at the bureau…ever. It's just not a good idea."

Oh, I was pissed now. Royally.

"Well," I said, nodding my head slowly. "I can see why not getting into anything serious with someone at the bureau is a good idea. However, *fucking* everyone at the bureau seems like a *great* one. God, why didn't I think of that?" I gave him my best clueless look, "I guess I must've been absent the day you went over that one."

He shrugged and nodded. "I thought you knew the score, doll. I mean, it's not like I ever took you out on a date or anything. I figured you understood what this was about."

Fuck you.

48

"Why don't you call Lisa back, Darin? Let her know your schedule for tonight has just been freed up."

I grabbed my purse from the sofa, and he made no move whatsoever to stop me.

"Cocksucker," I breathed out on a harsh breath, as I pushed the door of his apartment open, taking the tattered remnants of my pride with me.

Chapter 6

I was perched on the sofa in the family room, spooning the last mouthful of Ben & Jerry's Cherry Garcia ice cream into my mouth, tossing the empty container onto the coffee table, where it joined its empty brother, 'Chunky Monkey' who'd gone first, when I heard Cain and Eli come in.

Shit! I just knew I was going to hear about eating up two containers of their precious ice cream. You see, I almost never indulged in that sort of thing anymore, which is why I never bought any for myself. Which is why, in crisis, I'd gotten into theirs.

You see, my boys were extremely territorial about their stuff and about my getting into it.

They had both mini-lectured me on using up their laundry detergent, borrowing their razors to shave my legs when I had run out of my disposable Lady Schicks (Cain had really been pissed about *that* one, knocking on my bedroom door with little bits of Kleenex tissue dotted with blood attached to his face, and chewing my ass out about it). So getting into their groceries was a major infraction for sure.

I braced myself for my next ass-chewing, as they came into the family room, having heard the television blaring some Lifetime flick I'd turned on. Lifetime's movie theme just happened to be "Eating Disorder Weekend."

And I'm not going to lie. Watching Meredith Baxter as some soccer mom with bulimia, shoveling ice cream into her mouth, as she placed her order for two large fries, a cheeseburger, a fish sandwich and two milk shakes at a drive-thru window was enough to get me into the mood for some comfort food.

They stopped short when they saw me, quickly assessing the situation.

"What happened?" Eli asked, standing in the entryway wearing nylon shorts and some kickass Nike's. "Why are you home so early?"

I didn't have time to even respond to his questions when Cain spoke up. "And *why* are you binge-eating Ben & Jerry's?"

"Yeah, about that, guys. Look, I'll replace those when I go to the grocery, I promise."

"We're not fucking worried about *that*," Eli said, coming over and plopping down next to me on the sofa. "Is everything okay?"

Cain was standing there silently with his arms crossed, waiting for an answer.

"Everything's good," I lied. "I just don't think that Darin and I will be seeing each other *socially* anymore. No biggie."

"What did that fuck do?" Cain asked, a humming anger in his voice as he sat down on the other side of me.

His dark eyes seemed to get even darker as he gazed at me, waiting for some explanation that I really didn't feel like putting out there to them. It was actually kind of embarrassing.

"It's nothing like *that*," I replied with a shrug. "It seems that he's not ready for anything exclusive, which is fine. I just wasn't aware of the rules, I guess. And now I am, so hey, it's all good. No harm, no foul."

"Asshat," Eli muttered under his breath. "Are you okay, babe?" I felt his arm wrap around me, pulling me closer to him.

"I'm fine, Eli. I'm really fine. It wasn't as if I was in love with him or anything like that."

My words sounded empty, like maybe there was no conviction behind them. "Look, I'm gonna call it a night," I told them, as I swept the empty ice-cream containers into one arm. "I'm still helping you with that reception tomorrow, right Cain?"

He pulled me away from Eli, forcing me to face him as he studied me. "If you don't feel like helping with that, it's okay, sweetie. I can get Debbie to come in."

"Don't be silly," I said, leaning over and giving his handsome face a Cherry Garcia-flavored kiss. "I need the extra jack, you know? I've got some ice cream to replace."

I turned from him and gave Eli a kiss on his cheek. "Night guys," I said, heading towards the kitchen. "See y'all in the morning."

Later in the privacy of my room, I quickly changed into my nightgown and brushed my teeth, not wanting to look at my reflection in the mirror.

The truth was that I was ashamed of myself for daring to let my guard down with a man. I very seldom had done that, maybe just once or twice before, and it had never worked out.

Why in the hell had I thought that Darin was going to be any different?

As I snuggled down under my sheets, I remembered what my last semi-boyfriend had told me when we parted. "You're just too hard to keep up with Paige. You want it all and I'm not willing to give it all just yet. You're not my idea of soul mate material. I'm sorry."

That had been Ryan; a guy that I'd known all through school, but hadn't dated until I got out of college. We had been seeing each other steadily for three months when he broke it off. He said I was getting too intense, whatever that meant. He had been the deciding factor in my coming to D.C. to find a career and, hopefully, a new beginning somewhere else.

It seemed as if my luck with men was destined to follow me wherever I went.

I didn't really understand it, though, because I sure wasn't big on the whole 'Let's get married' or 'Let's live together' thing. I was simply looking for some intimacy—a connection that was more than just good sex, something that complimented the sex, that made it more than just a physical thing, but not an ownership thing, either. Somewhere in the middle, I guess.

The best relationship I had going was the one I had with these men. How screwed up was that?

Eli and Cain were the closest thing to soul mates that I'd ever had, even though we hadn't really been a threesome for all that long.

And the fucked-up thing about that was that they were gay and in love and devoted to one another. How could I possibly fit into that equation?

But somehow, they *did* make me feel as if I belonged with them; like they cared about me as a woman, not as baby sister like it was with Trace and Easton.

And *that* part of it was what helped me get through stuff like this. Darin the asshat…Eli was so on the mark with that one. I sighed, somehow feeling comforted by these men that I lived with.

Chapter 7

Cain and I were unpacking all of the linens, china, crystal and silverware for the wedding reception that he was catering. This one happened to be in the basement underneath the church where the wedding was taking place.

"Paige, if you set up the tables, I'm going to get the coffee service going, okay?"

"Sure," I replied, straightening out the white tablecloth at the wedding party table. "Who's setting the bar up?"

"Dry reception," he remarked, as he backed through the swinging door to the kitchen, waggling his eyebrows. "Sorry babe, I know you love the tips."

That sucks.

I enjoyed working with Cain and the others at these receptions, but the most enjoyable ones were those that had a bar set up. Cain usually allowed me to work the bar and the tips were pretty substantial.

A couple of the other girls had pissed and moaned a bit because they were full-time employees, not a fill-in like I was when one of the other workers wanted a Saturday off. Cain had explained his rationale to them: He was the boss, and if they didn't like it, then fucking go somewhere else.

Bahahaha!!

Jake and Connie came in; rolling a cart that had the wedding cake and punch bowl on it.

"Damn," I said, wrinkling my nose, "How big is this reception? That cake looks like it could feed a hundred people."

I looked around and saw that the tables were set up for about forty people max, not counting the wedding party which was set for six.

"Hah," Jake snorted with a smile, "Just wait until you see the newlyweds." I shrugged and continued with arranging the place settings.

Cain returned with the silver coffee service, Styrofoam cups along with the cream and sugar packets. "This is going to be a hot and cold appetizer buffet, Paige. So when you're finished up with the tables, can you give Julie some help getting the food table set up?"

"Sure thing, sweetie," I replied, tossing him a smile.

I had worked enough of these things to know the signs by now. This was a 'no-frills' reception. First clue: Booze-less. Second clue: an appetizer buffet that consisted of miniature pigs-in-a-blanket, chicken wings, deviled eggs (sans Cayenne pepper) potato salad, baked beans and potato chips.

We had barely gotten everything into place and the punch bowl filled, when the door to the church basement opened, and guests started piling in. The wedding party was close behind and then I got it.

Oh dear Lord.

The bride and groom had to have a combined weight of over six hundred pounds. The rest of the wedding party wasn't far behind. Thus the reason for the 7-tiered wedding cake, I presumed.

Music streamed through speakers placed around the room from a Spotify playlist of traditional love songs for weddings. I watched as the bride and groom interacted with one another and their guests. I hadn't realized that Cain had come up behind me as I released a wistful sigh.

"Something wrong?" he asked, placing his hands on my shoulders, startling me a bit, and then massaging them back into relaxation.

I shrugged, and then nodded slightly. "Look at them, Cain," I said softly, "Their love for one another is so beautiful and, I don't know, it kind of makes them look beautiful to me, you know?"

"Well who would've thought that our Paige was such a closet romantic?" he teased. "Wait until I share this with Eli."

"Oh stop," I said, smacking him playfully. "I've got no ax to grind with romance; romance just seems to have an ax to grind with me, I guess."

"Why would you say that?" he questioned, pulling me around to face him. "Is this about that fucking idiot, Darin?"

His eyes were once again piercing through me. Cain was so freaking intense sometimes that it gave me chills. I shivered, and his hands were quick to rub my back and shoulders gently, but he was still waiting for an answer.

"No—it's not about *him*," I replied. "It's more about me. I mean, is there something about me—some sort of repulse pheromone I'm giving off? Never mind—you aren't exactly the demographic I'm looking for anyway."

Shit.

I saw the fire flash in his eyes at the comment. I hadn't meant it like that...exactly. I mean, what the hell? Posing a question like that to a gay dude wasn't exactly fair, was it?

"Outside, now," he ordered, taking me by the arm and pulling me alongside of him. "You and I need to take a break."

Once outside, Cain found a concrete bench off to the side of the church, in a grassy area that had a statue of the Blessed Mother behind it.

"Sit," he ordered.

I sat down, waiting for him to take a seat, but he remained standing.

"First of all, sweetheart, you need to shed some of your pre-conceived notions about alternative lifestyles. Contrary to what you seem to think, homosexuals and bisexuals all don't fall into one neat little category that is black and white, okay?"

I nodded, and started to speak, but he raised his hand, his index finger pointing at me to remain quiet.

"Secondly, you've been with Eli and me long enough that we've both seen what you're doing. We've discussed it amongst ourselves, to be honest."

I quirked an eyebrow, hoping like hell that he intended to clue me in on their assessment.

"Paige," he sighed, "You are bright and beautiful and sexy as fuck, don't you get that? But—what we see in you is the *need* you have to treat men as either total sex objects, with which to pleasure yourself at leisure—and granted, this information is second-hand from Darcy through Lindsey, but when you *do* try to focus on something more substantive, you select the type of guy that isn't game for anything *but* leisure sex. And *that* is first-hand knowledge from our own observation. Baby, you seem to set yourself up for failure all around."

I was thoughtful for a moment, reflecting upon his words, knowing that he was onto me. Eli too. They hadn't been fooled one little bit. I was a hot mess.

"So, babe, to answer your question in there? No. You're not putting out some 'repulse' pheromone. And whether I'm bisexual or not, I would know, just as Eli knows, you simply need to put yourself out there to the right guy and there won't be a doubt in that pretty little head of yours when it's right."

"You're bisexual?" I asked, swallowing hard. "I mean…does Eli know?"

He threw his head back and I heard his deep, rich laugh, something that was rare with Cain. "Oh yeah, he knows. He's fine with it. Well, he's maybe more than fine with it, to be honest."

My eyebrows once again traveled up my forehead.

Cain continued, "Eli's bisexual as well—or maybe I should say he's a *closet* bi," he said, giving me a wink.

"It kind of came out in 'couples therapy,' and I swear to God if you tell him that I mentioned couples therapy, I'll fucking hunt you down," he warned, giving me a faux stern look.

"Really? Couples therapy?"

He rolled his eyes in a very delightful way, almost shy-like. "Yeah, we went through some…shit a while back. It's all good now, but we needed to bring things out into the open to build up our trust in one another. Eli had never told me that he had been married—very briefly—the summer before he went to college. Shocked the hell out of me," he said, shaking his head.

"So, why do you say he's a *closet* bi?"

I mean, what the hell? I'd heard of closet gays, but I pretty much thought bisexuals were out with it, if they went both ways like that.

"Well, although he finds members of both genders sexually appealing, he's made a choice to have only one sexual preference at the moment. He said chicks are too high-maintenance," he finished, giving me a cocky smile.

Oh. What. Ever.

"As if anyone would ever categorize Eli as being *low* maintenance," I scoffed absently.

This brought a smile from Cain as he stepped forward, drawing me into his arms. His hand gently brushed through my hair, and I felt his full lips graze my forehead, as I relaxed into his warm embrace. It was comforting and it felt right for some reason.

"All I want to tell you, Paige, is to stop hiding behind your dual facades," he murmured. "If you stop doing things for attention, and you start being who you're meant to be, I think your need for romance and commitment will be satisfied. Sometimes, it's right there in front of you."

He gave me a peck on the cheek, and released me from his grasp. "Now, come on, babe. We have a wedding cake to start slicing."

I watched him as I trailed behind him, feeling a warm, fluttery feeling in the pit of my belly as I contemplated his words.

'Sometimes it's right there in front of you...'

Was there some hidden meaning in his words, or was I simply reading too much into his kindness and concern?

I would never do anything to hurt Eli, no matter how close Cain and I had become over the past couple of months. And then again, what had Cain meant when he said that Eli was 'more than fine with it'? Did that mean that Eli...?

Too many questions; too few answers. I was totally confused. I needed to hook up. I knew exactly what was going to be on my agenda tonight.

Chapter 8

"That's it, baby. Good girl. Take it all."

I squeezed my eyes shut tightly, as Travis buried his long, thick, sheathed cock into me, backed out, and then plunged it in again deeply, grunting his pleasure.

Travis?

Maybe his name is actually Trevor...*what the fuck. Who cares?*

"Does it feel good, baby? Do you like the feel of Trevor's cock ramming into your pussy like this, huh?"

It's Trevor...right. Random Trevor, referring to himself in the third person. Lovely.

"Yeah, baby," I murmured. "You're the fucking best," I lied, wishing he'd get his nut, because I sure as hell wasn't going to get mine with this ass-hat.

The problem was, he totally had a Bud-Lite hard-on going, and I knew that meant it would be a while before he came.

"That's right, baby," he whispered, groaning and smothering my lips with wet, beer-flavored kisses. "You're going to scream when Trevor makes you come."

Seriously?

Aannd...that's a wrap.

"Get the fuck off of me," I finally said, before clamping my mouth shut and turning my head away from him. "Now," I said, louder.

He stopped his thrusting momentarily, as if my words weren't totally registering in his drunken brain. He didn't pull out of me though, and I was getting really pissed.

"Did you hear me?" I yelled, using my hands to push against his chest, trying to get his long, muscular frame off of me.

"What the fuck?" he asked, loudly. "I ain't goin' nowhere just yet," he remarked, shifting his weight so that my hands were smashed between the both of us as he continued humping me.

"I said stop!" I screamed as loudly as possible. "I want you out of me and out of here!" I yelled into his left ear.

"Fuckin' bitch," he growled, fisting my hair so that my head snapped back.

I thrashed around underneath him, my legs getting twisted up in the sheets, my fists pummeling against his bare chest.

"I said get off of me," I shouted.

Suddenly, I heard my bedroom door open and slam loudly against the wall, startling Trevor enough that his unwelcome thrusting stopped.

In seconds flat, his weight was lifted off of me, and he was slammed unceremoniously against my bedroom wall, where he slid the rest of the way down into a naked heap on the floor.

It was Cain. He was pissed…dark eyes flashing, his fists clenched at his side.

"You have about two fucking seconds to get the *fuck* out of here," Cain growled out the quiet threat, "Before I reinvent the term, *blue balls*. Got me?"

Eli was there now as well, rubbing the sleep from his eyes, and wearing nothing but cotton sweats and a concrete look of concern.

I scurried out of the bed, gripping the white sheets around my scantily-clad form and watched as Trevor ineptly got to his feet with *no* sheet and a deflated hard-on.

Eli, now entirely awake, helped him find his clothes by tossing them at him. And if denim could ever give a person a black eye, I'm pretty sure that's what they did as Trevor not-so-successfully tried to catch his pants.

I watched as Eli gripped Trevor's arm just as he was zipping up and began to lead him out of the room.

"Get the fuck off me, fag!" Trevor wrenched his arm free.

"Yeah…," I heard Eli reply as he shoved Trevor through the open door, "Not goin' to happen, asshole."

Their heavy steps down the stairs and Trevor's drunken insults were the only sound in the 2 a.m. house as I stood there still staring at the door, trying to process the rapid chain of events that just went down.

Hoooly shit!

I looked over at the other person in the room, "Cain, I'm so sor—"

"Give me a minute." He cut me off, not even looking in my direction as his hands were settled on his hips, and he sucked in a deep breath, looking down at the floor.

My mouth immediately closed. I had never heard Cain yell, and never even *once* saw the guy lose his shit. So, the fact that he was looking a little like the Hulk standing there in his Metallica T-shirt and black-striped PJ bottoms, meant I'm pretty sure I would've given him the entire night to get his cool mojo back.

He looked up, and pinned me down with his dark eyes and a black look. Instantly, I shifted my sheet up a little higher. His eyes followed the movement, and I saw his jaw clench.

"That's not going to help," Cain said, warningly.

I shrugged, "Look, it's not that big of a deal."

He responded by giving me one hell of a wry look before asking, "Is *this* what you do?"

I stood up a bit straighter, "Excuse me?"

"Take guys home. Let them fuck you in your own bedroom, even when you tell them no," he deadpanned. "*Is this what you do?*"

"No!" I exclaimed. What the hell was he talking about?

"Then what just happened," he took a step towards me, "is a *big* fucking deal, Paige."

"He just got carried away. I would have handled it," I told him, probably trying to convince the both of us.

Cain was about a foot from where I was standing now, and he was just about to take another step forward when Eli came walking in.

"Okay, the trash has officially been taken out," he announced, a bit ceremoniously.

Cain shook his head and began to retreat towards the door, but not before tossing back the words, "We'll talk in the morning, Paige."

I looked over at Eli for help. But he had nothing to give me except for, "Yeah, you fucked up." He made his way over to an exit from this overly dramatic scene, "Bad."

And with that, the door closed.

This…wasn't good.

∞∞∞∞∞∞∞∞∞∞∞∞∞∞∞∞∞∞∞∞∞∞∞∞∞∞∞∞∞

I felt as if I were back in junior high school.

Perched on a kitchen chair, Eli leaning back against the counter, arms crossed staring at me, while Cain was standing in front of me, hands once again on his hips, sort of glaring, while they both took turns verbally laying out the ground rules to me.

"Last night can't happen again," Cain started off, leaning in a bit to make sure I knew that he was dead-ass serious.

"Yes," I nodded, putting a bit of meekness into my voice for sincerity.

"Jesus, Paige, what *was* that?" Eli quipped in.

I met Cain's gaze before focusing all of my attention onto Eli. Yeah, I already knew that my day was shot. Waking up to these two and having to go through drinking my coffee in utter silence was definitely not my idea of starting out a good day.

What really put the emphasis on the whole morning suckage, was the fact that I didn't have an answer for either of them.

Should I have brought Trevor back here last night? Probably not.

Did I possibly have way too much to drink last night? Probably yes.

What would have happened if Cain and Eli didn't come in with their super-dude capes? I didn't even want to *think* about the answer to that one.

"Paige?" Eli said my name again, trying to regain my focus on the issue at hand.

"I get it," I told the both of them, crossing my arms and probably coming off as a petulant child.

But, shit! These guys held all the cards right now, and this could all play out in a million ways. And I damn well wasn't going to gamble by giving them an answer I wasn't sure about.

Another moment of silence.

Clearly, when they saw I wasn't going to give them the speech about how last night happened and why, Eli switched tactics. "It's not about the sex."

What?

"It's about judging character," Eli continued.

"Uhh...well, if you're saying that I should have seen what happened coming, then—"

"That's exactly what I'm saying," Eli deadpanned.

Okay. I was struggling with the decision of either giving him a *WTF?* look...or the finger. Because I, honest to God, didn't know how in the hell I could have possibly known that Trevor was going to go all "The Accused" on me.

"Okay," I said, getting up from the chair. "If you guys are seriously trying to convey that I asked for that last night, then screw you both."

I started to walk off when I felt a hand on my arm. Turning around, prepared to give one hell of a verbal lashing, I was surprised to see that it was Cain who had the vise-like hold on me.

"That's not what he's saying," Cain explained, meeting my gaze. I looked down to where he was holding me, and he let go.

"Then what *is* he saying?" I didn't even spare Eli a glance as I kept my eyes padlocked to Cain's.

"He's saying that you should always pick someone who…takes care of you." Cain took a step back, now looking over at Eli, who was nodding his head.

"I don't follow."

Eli tossed the remains of what was in his coffee cup into the sink before turning around to face me.

"Trevor Mulroney always has a breath mint and at least six condoms at hand. He doesn't give two shits about the women he sleeps with, because all he can think about is getting some. I mean, the guy doesn't even *care* if the women he's sleeping with get off. It might as well be rape even if it is consensual because they're just a breathing pocket-pussy as far as he's concerned. Something to use."

"Well, how was I supposed to know *that?*" I asked, my eyes darting between them both. Although in all honesty, wasn't that exactly what I'd gone after? I was used to being used; I was used to using right back. For whatever reason, I sucked at cultivating relationships. Being "used" was my comfort zone.

Eli was just about to respond, when Cain beat him to it.

"You should have taken the time to know that," he said softly, like this was a conversation just between the two of us. "You deserve respect, and in order to understand that, maybe a little self-respect is what you need the most."

I nodded slowly, my eyes drifting down to the kitchen tile. I felt a gentle hand come up to my jaw, and raise my head up to meet a pair of russet-colored eyes.

"You have to learn to respect yourself," Cain told me with gentle brutality, his hand still holding my face. "Sexuality isn't a privilege or a lifestyle, Paige. It's a person's *right*. You can do anything you want to do with…whomever. But you have to respect yourself, and make sure that the other person damn well respects you too."

I let those words churn over in my mind a little before I even thought about responding. Letting out a breath that I didn't even realize I had been holding, I made sure to meet both of their gazes straight-on. He was right. *They* were right. I had a long way to go, but it wouldn't be any shorter if I continued on this self-destructive path.

"I'm sorry." I genuinely confessed. "I know that you're both right. I'll work on it, I promise."

Chapter 9

It had been nearly four months since that awful episode with Trevor and my men hosting their "come to Jesus" meeting with me. Since then, I had worked my ass off, both at the academy, and at home. And I had fought the temptation for any further random hook-ups, which I found was much easier if I wore myself out physically.

So that's what I did, both in the gym, at home, and with Cain.

Let me explain. I helped Cain every chance I got with his catering business. It was a win-win because not only did I earn some extra cash, but I stayed out of trouble. Little by little I started banking some self-respect along the way.

I was pretty sure that I had earned both Cain and Eli's respect in the meantime, if I hadn't had it before. I think they had been genuinely concerned about me—they cared about me and, in return, I had this unfamiliar need to please them. That was a first for me.

I paid off my car, and had some additional spending money, which I put to good use, sprucing up my wardrobe, and buying some decorative things for the house, determined that it would have my signature style right along with theirs. After all, we were all in this thing together. It felt good to belong somewhere, and I knew that I did.

I had kept a professional attitude where Darin was concerned. I mean, after all, he was still my superior and I needed to make sure that I kept everything above reproach.

Besides, I really had no ax to grind with him. Everything he had said to me that evening had been true. Any inkling of a committed relationship had been in my own mind. I couldn't hold him responsible for leading me on because he really hadn't.

We were getting the house prepped for the holidays. Eli had made plans to spend Thanksgiving with Darcy and Easton; Trace and Lindsey were spending Thanksgiving with Lindsey's side of the family. Cain and I had been invited to Darcy's as well, but Cain had a major catering gig and I had offered my help.

And it wasn't as if Thanksgiving was that big of a deal to me anyway.

Now Christmas?

Yeah, that was another story. I had already brought up the artificial Christmas tree from the basement, along with the multiple boxes of decorations.

I had enlisted my men's help in rearranging the living room furniture so that our tree could be placed in front of the picture window, so all who traveled down our street could see it, once it was decorated, in all of its eclectic and electric magnificence.

My guys told me that once Thanksgiving had passed, we could get the tree and the outside lights that I had bought put up.

Cain and I got through catering the banquet at one of the local country clubs. Once home, we were exhausted, so we flopped down on the sofa for a breather.

"You did well tonight, Paige," he complimented. "You're a damn good worker. I appreciate your jumping in to help out, being that a couple of my *trusted* employees called off last minute. I like that I can depend on you."

I looked over at him, my head resting against the back of the sofa. "It means a lot to me that you said that," I said with a sigh. "I'm not going to lie, though. It was a bitch today, Cain."

He nodded with a loud laugh on his lips and a silent one in his eyes.

It always took me completely off-guard when Cain laughed. I mean yeah, I knew that the guy was human…but when there was a smile on his face; he went from a brooding man to a boyish, sexy guy. It was friggin' disarming, and I never fully knew how to react and keep the moment when it happened.

I didn't even realize that I had probably been staring for a full-on minute when Cain looked over at me, a smaller smile hanging from his face. "You're doing that staring thing again," he teased.

My eyebrows crept together at that comment, "What staring thing?"

He let out another small laugh, and I kind of wanted to throw it in my pocket.

"That staring thing you do when you don't think I'm paying attention," Cain explained.

"Umm...I think *someone* needs to get his ego checked," I nudged him playfully in the arm. "One, I don't stare. And two, even if I *did*, what makes you think I'd waste it on someone who looks like they spend their spare time running over baby bunnies?" For bonus effect, I raised one eyebrow.

I watched his eyes widen as he looked at me, right before he threw his head back and let out a deep, rich laugh. He looked back over, "Baby bunnies? Where the hell do you even get this stuff?"

Waggling my eyebrows, I shrugged. "T.V."

He snorted, and I turned fully so that my body was facing his entirely now. "No, seriously. T.V. can teach you a *lot* of things, my friend. For instance, when I was fourteen and I heard that Billy Jameson wanted to kiss me, I watched Beverly Hills 90210 for a solid afternoon."

"And...?" Cain asked, with questioning eyes.

"Aaaand, not only did I learn how to kiss...," I paused dramatically, before gesturing him to come closer, as if I planned on telling him my biggest, darkest secret. When he complied, I brought my face super close to his and whispered mischievously, "I learned how to *French*."

Exuberant shock took over his features, and that earlier smile built a home in his voice as he asked, "And what did this Billy think?"

"Well," I replied, tossing my hair back and having fun with this game we were playing. "He thought that I kissed *way* better than the sophomore girls."

"Did he?"

It was such a quiet question. And for some reason, the low way Cain spoke those words were beginning to crack through the innocence of the moment we had just shared.

Our faces were still close together when I managed a small nod, a new kind of moment shocking through the lessening space between us.

His lips grazed mine first, and it was such a soft feeling that I knew if I had blinked, I wouldn't have even felt it.

Until he gave me a second one.

This time, he ran his lips back and forth across mine, as if asking some arbitrary question. Looking back at that moment, I knew that I should've stopped it.

Ended it.

Started it on fire.

Torn it to shreds so that later, I could delve into the trash can and piece it all back together.

Instead, I sucked in a demanding breath and took his bottom lip between mine. Biting down lightly, I heard him softly growl right before feeling his hand lightly gripping the nape of my neck.

And that's when he decided to throw gasoline on his next kiss.

Cain pulled my head back slightly, and then completely took over. His mouth softly worked mine at first, until I took another breath, and then he used that to his advantage, as his tongue stole in and caressed over mine.

Jesus, he tastes fucking awesome.

It was a mixture of mint and honey, and fuck me…I wanted a lot more.

Bringing my arms up to grip his biceps, I leaned in and took back the advantage as I found a new angle for his mouth. Kissing him and sucking hard on his tongue, I felt his hands grip the skin that showed above my low-slung pants.

And then I was being flipped over.

I found myself on my back, and Cain now had the advantage again as he settled over me and brought my arms up above my head.

He looked down at me with heat in his eyes that was threatening to singe his eyelashes. I was practically panting as he leaned back down and nipped at my ear, right before quietly sucking on the sensitive skin behind.

"He was right," he whispered.

I couldn't help it, I giggled as I turned my head to look at him. "Better than a sophomore?"

He gave me a small smile before leaning in and kissing me with whole lot of sexual aggression, to the point where it was almost punishing.

"Better than *anyone*," he practically growled, right before nipping the corner of my lips.

And that's when we heard the sound of Eli's car in the drive. Cain and I glanced at one other, and the shards of reality dusted over us as we immediately got as far away from each as the few seconds would allow.

Seriously, what the fuck just happened?

Just then, Eli came through the door, his arms full of Tupperware containers and foil-wrapped items.

"Got plenty of leftovers for my favorite peeps," he chimed in, clearly having imbibed in some holiday spirits. "Want to make sure you two got your holiday feast, being that you both spent the day serving it up to everyone else."

Cain jumped up from the couch, off-loading Eli of some of the containers, and following him into the kitchen. "Uh, Eli…did Darcy cook?"

I heard Eli's good-natured laugh float out from the kitchen. "Don't worry, it's all good," he chuckled. "Paige? Get your perky ass in here. I'm making you a plate," he hollered out.

I went into the kitchen where Eli was setting down clean plates and silverware. Cain was busy opening the containers of food, and putting them in the microwave to heat. I grabbed a bottle of Chardonnay from the wine chiller and dug for the corkscrew in the kitchen drawer.

"So how was everything over at 'Matthews Manor'?" I asked, twisting the corkscrew, anxious for any type of conversation to take my mind off of 'Kissing-Gate 2014' that had just gone down not even five minutes before. I so didn't want to relapse back to my skank days. I had too much to lose with these men.

"Big announcement this afternoon," Eli said, using his faux British accent.

He placed a folded hand towel over his arm, taking the open wine bottle from me, and filled my wine glass as a proper servant would. "Yes, mum. It seems Lady Darcy is in a delicate condition. She will be presenting his lordship with their second born next April. The Lord of the Manor has made it quite clear his preference is for a daughter this time."

I looked up into Eli's amused eyes. He was actually kind of good at impersonating Easton's accent. "Seriously? She's pregnant?"

"Yep," he said, his grin now fading. "They're pretty pumped up about it. Lucky them, I guess," he finished with a wistful sigh.

I looked over at him a tad confused. I noticed Cain had turned from the microwave to glance over at him as well. Our eyes locked briefly, before I turned my attention back to Eli.

"Aren't you happy for them, Eli?" I asked softly, placing my hand over his.

He looked up and painted a smile back on for my benefit. "What? Oh, sure I am. Just a bit jealous maybe. The closer I get to thirty, the more appealing the whole minivan-and-soccer-practice life looks."

I hadn't considered that with these men. I mean, they were in love and as committed to one another as anyone could be—married or otherwise. It was natural I suppose they might have the same dreams as any other couple with respect to raising children.

"Here we go," Cain said, interrupting my thoughts and the now-saddened tension in the room as he placed containers of warmed food on the table. "Dig in."

Later, as Cain and I finished cleaning up the kitchen, and Eli was taking out the trash, I brought the subject up. I had all but forgotten about the kiss as this new topic moved to the top.

"Do you and Eli want children, Cain?"

He looked over at me, caught off-guard momentarily. He shrugged and gave a small nod.

"Yeah, we've looked into it," he admitted. "You think that's fucked up, don't you?"

I shook my head. "No, not really," I replied. "I guess until I just now saw how Eli reacted to Darcy's news,

I hadn't really thought about it. I've never heard you guys discuss it."

"Well, you're not privy to *every* conversation we have, Paige. You know, we do manage to have private discussions when *possible*," he replied, trying to throw some humor into his words. Clearly, it was his polite way of saying, 'MYOB.'

Cool. No problemo.

I turned to leave the kitchen, and felt his hand on my arm, pulling me around to face him. His eyes were warm and soft now, a hint of remorse lacing his expression.

"Hey, I'm sorry," he replied gently. "I didn't mean to snap at you like that. It's kind of a sore subject, I guess. It's the one thing we can't give one another and it's frustrating as hell. We aren't on the same page with it, in all honesty."

"S'alright," I said with a nod, turning to leave.

"Hey you two," Eli said, coming into the kitchen. "Want to play some cards or something?"

I gave Eli a kiss on the cheek as I headed out. "I'm exhausted guys, rain check? This chick has a date with a long soak in a tub full of bubbles. Don't forget—tomorrow we start decorating inside and out."

I heard their manly grumbles as I retreated down the hallway to my room.

My bubble bath was delicious. I soaked for nearly an hour, and thought about the kiss Cain had given me. Maybe I was making too much of it. Maybe it was just something done without thought. I was inclined to believe that's all it was.

I mean, we all cared for each other; that was perfectly clear. We were all close, so maybe it didn't have to mean a damn thing. I wasn't going to overanalyze it. I probably needed to get out more. I'd kind of become a house frau and it was showing. I hadn't sworn off men for life, just the users. Maybe I was ready to try my hand at cultivating a real relationship with someone who had potential rather than just anyone with a hard dick.

After my bath, I climbed into my empty bed and pulled out the large plastic bag that contained yarn, knitting needles and the two work-in-progress wool scarves I'd been knitting in secret for a couple of weeks.

I was making a dark teal scarf for Eli; Cain's was a dark maroon, and I couldn't help but laugh a bit when it sort of/probably looked an awful lot like something Draco Malfoy would wear. The colors were perfect for each of their palettes.

My Grandmother Townsend (my mom's mother) had taught me how to knit and crochet one summer when I stayed at her house in Oregon. I was probably eleven or twelve at the time. She lived in the middle of nowhere, so I had been happy to have something to keep me busy.

I had knitted potholders of every color, and crocheted hats for my parents and brother, proudly presenting them as gifts when I arrived back home. Only, I never saw my mother use that first potholder, and of course, the hats hadn't really been their style I was told.

The following year, my Grandmother Townsend passed away. When my mother returned home after her burial, she brought boxes of yarn, knitting needles, crochet hooks, and patterns with her and gave them to me.

Over the years, I had dabbled here and there with making things. It was a skill that had stuck with me, I suppose, and would serve me well in making Christmas presents for my guys.

I had found earmuffs on sale to go with them. My budget was still fairly tight these days.

I was knitting away, finding the sound of the clicking needles almost soothing. My grandmother had told me that many a problem had found a solution while she knitted. Maybe I'd have a better chance of finding a date if I wasn't sitting home knitting, I thought to myself with a smile.

I definitely needed to do something before New Year's Eve, because this girl, as mature and down-to-earth as she was trying to be, wasn't going to be a fucking wallflower on New Year's Eve.

There had been a couple of guys at the bureau who worked in Accounting that had been somewhat flirtatious with me, but I'd pretty much been blowing them off.

I promised myself that, after Thanksgiving, I would make a concerted effort to strike up a conversation with one of them. They were both very nice guys, and not the usual bad-boy types I seemed to gravitate towards. That had to be a good sign. I'd start with Kenneth. He had the higher-level position of the two.

I smiled as I continued knitting. Granny Townsend was right. I had definitely worked out a practical plan while knitting, to ensure I was on the right path toward maturity, self-respect and cultivating healthy relationships.

Chapter 10

We all had Black Friday off from our respective jobs, so I put the guys to work assembling the Douglas Fir artificial tree, and getting the white twinkle lights situated evenly. That had managed to get me several exasperated sighs and a couple of eye rolls thrown my way.

I admit, I was damn picky when it came to my Christmas tree decorating. My mother had always left it for me to do, once Trace left home, and I had taken the responsibility quite seriously.

"Much better, Eli," I praised, after I had instructed him to fill the gap where one string of lights plugged into the next.

"Thank you, Princess Paige," he teased, with a shake of his head. "Damn, I never knew how inept I was at this until you so graciously pointed out the multiple faux pas I made here." He gave a waggle of his eyebrows.

Cain came in from the garage just then with another rubber tub marked "X-MAS SHIT." He set it down next to the tree and took the lid off of it.

"Here it is," he said, with a big smile. "I knew we hadn't tossed this stuff out before the move."

He reached in and pulled out several home-made ornaments. Like maybe from his own childhood. There were snowmen and gingerbread men made out of colored felt, with sequins and buttons glued on, a Christmas angel that looked like it had been made out of a tampon, with a bunch of glitter adorning it and a gold pipe-cleaner shaped as the wings.

"These are precious," I said, my lips twitching to a smile. I had never seen Cain look like a 'kid at Christmas' which was exactly how he looked at this very moment. It was hard to even imagine him being a child, what with his serious nature and the passionate undercurrent I had felt first-hand the night before.

He looked over at me and our eyes met.

Damn, he was fucking complicated—or maybe it was simply that the longer I knew him, the less I seemed to know him. He could still surprise me with his sudden change of emotions, or the occasional peek into his psyche.

"I don't know why I've kept these," he admitted with a sheepish smile. "I guess it's the fact that they represent some happy times as a kid."

"Or because you're an insufferable packrat," Eli chimed in, as he started hanging Christmas ornaments. He didn't catch the one finger salute Cain threw up behind his back, giving me a wink.

I started putting wire hooks into some of Cain's ornaments, getting ready to hang them. "Where did you grow up, Cain?"

"Chicago," he replied. "Until my parents divorced when I was thirteen, then I moved with my mother to Baltimore. I didn't see my father much after that," he said, shrugging.

I knew Cain well enough by now not to dig any deeper. If he wanted me to know more, he would tell me when he was ready. Compared to Eli and me, just from the bits and pieces that Cain had shared over the past several months, his formative years didn't sound particularly pleasant.

We were nearly finished trimming the tree when Eli looked at his watch. "Shit, I'm fifteen minutes late picking up Darce."

"Huh?" I asked, looking over at him as he headed for the closet.

"Shopping. We made plans yesterday."

"You're actually going out with all of the crazies on the worst fucking shopping day of the year?" I asked incredulously.

Cain snorted. "You know better than to ask, Paige. Dude doesn't miss a chance to out-shop Darcy."

"Yeah, as if," Eli chuckled, zipping up his jacket. "I'll stop on the way home for some Chinese take-out. Sound good?"

"Fine by me," I replied, placing an ornament on the tree. "Be careful out there."

Cain and I finished the tree, making small talk about our Christmases growing up. I felt a bit uncomfortable, like something was hanging over our heads that we weren't addressing. I finally had enough nerve to mention it.

"Cain, I know that you're a private person and I totally respect that, but you and I need to talk about yesterday...about the kiss." I was stumbling over my words, not sure what his reaction would be.

He slowly nodded. "I know," he said, softly. "I hope I didn't totally freak you out. I just couldn't resist," he finished.

I sat up straighter as he appeared to collect his thoughts. I also made sure that there was a decent amount of couch between us this time.

"I'm drawn to you," he said, as if we were just two people talking about the weather. "Sexually...and emotionally."

When he just tossed that out there, I probably looked like some sort of a fish in shock because I felt my eyes widen... but words eluded me.

He continued, "Eli knows it. I told him last night about the kiss," Cain let out a small laugh. "And he's not upset; he's not even surprised."

"I guess I'm confused," I murmured. "I don't want to cause problems between the two of you. You *do* know that I care deeply for both of you, right?"

He nodded, giving me a trace of a smile. "I do know that—we *both* know that. Hey, I'm sorry if I made you uncomfortable with that, Paige. I just needed to put it out there, because it's just who I am and it's how I feel."

I wasn't sure how I felt about it now, knowing that he had told Eli and, for whatever reason, Eli had understood. This was all very new ground for me. I opted to change the subject for now.

"You know," I said, "There's a guy at work that's kind of been flirting with me the past couple of months."

I saw Cain quirk an eyebrow, but he remained silent.

"Anyway," I continued, "You can rest assured he's not the…caliber I went for in the past. I've learned my lesson on that, thanks to you guys. So, would it be okay if I invited him here for dinner…maybe next week?"

Cain eyed me warily, his eyes narrowing infinitesimally. "This is your home too, Paige. You don't need our permission to have a guest for dinner."

I flushed, feeling a bit embarrassed. "I know *that*," I responded. "What I *meant* was that I'd like you and Eli to be here for dinner as well. So that, you know, you can meet Kenneth? We're sort of like family, the three of us. Especially since none of mine even seem to be talking to me much these days," I finished quietly.

"It's fine, Paige," Cain replied softly. "Just let us know when and we'll make sure to become the Italian mafia for the special occasion, alright?"

I smiled, feeling better already. I wanted these men to like any man I brought home for them to meet. I needed their seal of approval, for some strange reason. What they thought about me mattered.

Chapter 11

I gazed at the dining room table that was beautifully set. The water glasses were filled, the wine was breathing and my homemade lasagna was baking in the oven.

I returned to the kitchen, chopping up celery for my salad. I popped a piece of it into my mouth, just as I felt strong arms encircle me from behind, causing me to jump and let out a high-pitched shriek.

I heard Eli's playful laugh. "Sorry, sweetie," he said, releasing me. "I didn't mean to scare you."

"What the hell, Eli?" I said, trying to swallow the chunk of celery now lodged in my throat.

"You okay?" he asked, smacking me on the back. "Sorry, babe, the smell of your lasagna makes me do impetuous things," he winked.

"I'm fine," I said, rolling my eyes. "How about you put some of your energy into making the salad?" I suggested. "Where's Cain?"

Eli grabbed a paring knife and started peeling a carrot. "He's just getting out of the shower. Don't worry; I laid out clothes for him. Wouldn't want to bring shame to our best girl while she tries to impress Kevin."

"It's *Kenneth*," I told him for about the fifth time this week. "Kenneth," I annunciated.

"Got it, got it," he said. "So what's *Kenneth's* story?"

I checked the lasagna, and turned the oven down a bit. "Well, he's older than me, probably thirty-ish—"

"Ah-hah—geezers like us," he teased.

"Sort of," I replied with a smile. "Truthfully, Eli, he *is* kind of a serious guy, so maybe you can drop our usual banter down a notch or two? I mean the guy's an accountant, for Chrissake, so I think the word of the day is conservative."

"Conservative?" he quipped, "My fucking word of the day is 'mismatch'."

"Huh?"

"Why the hell would you pursue a relationship with a dude who you admit is a stuffy bean-counter?"

"I didn't say stuffy," I replied.

"It was *implied*, babe."

Just then, Cain came into the kitchen, dressed in the casual Dockers/Polo ensemble that Eli had selected for him.

"What the fuck smells so good?" he asked, his eyes widening.

"See," I snapped. "That's just what I mean." I tossed my hand up in the air in exasperation.

"Chill, Paige," Eli replied, and then directed his attention to the befuddled Cain. "It seems as though we need to act like we have couth and manners this evening,

Maddox. Paige just described Kenneth as being...well, *boring*."

I grabbed the wooden salad utensils from the counter and started tossing. "I didn't say boring; I said conservative. I mean, come on guys, I don't want him thinking I live with heathens, alright?"

"Hey, this is your gig, babe," Cain said. "We'll take our cue from you, how's that?"

"Perfect," I replied, taking the salad bowl out to the table.

∞∞∞∞∞∞∞∞∞∞∞∞∞∞∞∞∞∞∞∞∞∞∞∞∞∞∞∞∞∞

Well, to say that dinner went well would be...an all-out lie.

Fuck me.

What had I been thinking, inviting Kenneth over? And I won't say my guys didn't try to find some topic of interest to draw my date into some masculine conversation. I mean, my God, they had to have been exhausted by the time the meal was blessedly over.

First off, Kenneth had no interest whatsoever in sports—any sports.

He has no interest in music, traveling, the arts, television programs, or even current events—with the exception of the national debt, about which he rambled on non-stop for nearly twenty minutes.

He also had no tolerance for being referred to as "Kenny," which Eli managed to do several times, much to Kenneth's obvious chagrin.

Finally, Eli and Cain retired to their room to give Kenneth and me some privacy, which to be honest, I didn't want. The dude was flat out on my fucking nerves. In fact, he was running neck-and-neck with ol' Trevor Mulroney at this point.

"Would you like a refill on your wine?" I asked Kenneth as we sat staring at one another at the now-cleared dining room table.

"Certainly, thank you," he replied, holding his glass up.

I poured myself some as well, thinking maybe this guy would be a tad more tolerable if I were under the influence a bit.

"So, Paige," he said quietly, leaning in as if he wanted to tell me a secret. "Is it safe for me to presume that your...uh...roommates are queers?"

I nearly spewed my mouthful of merlot onto his crisply-ironed white oxford shirt. I grabbed a napkin, wiping my mouth as I managed to swallow it instead.

"Uh, Kenneth? Exactly *who* uses that word these days?" I asked, looking him dead in the eyes.

"I apologize," he replied, quickly. "Homos, then?"

Ah, fuck to the no...

"You know," I started, trying to choose my words carefully, "I guess I don't understand why the sexual preference of my roommates—who, by the way, are very close to me, would be of any consequence to you."

He looked a bit taken aback at being called out on his own ignorance and stupidity.

"Well, it's just that your living arrangement took me a bit by surprise. I mean, I've been trying to talk to you for months, but you didn't seem interested. Then, out of the blue, you invite me to dinner this week and introduce me to your roommates, whom you obviously wanted in attendance for our date. It just makes me wonder whether you don't feel comfortable being alone with me—or maybe if it's something else altogether."

What. The. Fuck?

"What do you mean by something else altogether?" I asked, not hiding my puzzlement at all.

I actually saw Kenneth squirm in his chair, and a blush appeared on his cheeks. "Well, uh, I am familiar with your reputation just a bit. I mean, well, Darin Murphy kind of likes to boast, know what I mean?"

I felt myself getting fired up at the mention of that douche's name. "Go on," I said firmly.

Kenneth was definitely out of his comfort zone now.

"Well, it's just that Darin kind of clued me in when I told him you had approached me for a dinner date at…your place. He told me about your roommates—and he may have asked something about my having experience with—uh…foursomes," he finished quickly. "I just want to tell you, right off the bat, that I'm not into any of that counter-culture stuff. It's got to be a one-on-one with you and me, okay?"

I was fairly sure my mouth was gaping open by this time, and my eyes were the size of saucers.

Yet still, he babbled on.

"I mean, when the time is right for you and me to have sexual intercourse, I would prefer that it be at my place—not here. I just don't think I could perform knowing that—"

So let me just stop right here and fast-forward.

Needless to say, Kenneth left our home before dessert was served. And when he left, there was no doubt in his mind that he'd never be back.

End of random date #1.

Chapter 12

It was four days before Christmas, and here I sat at one of the nicest restaurants this side of D.C., across from Roger Falconer.

I'd gone all-out getting dressed this evening in a black knit dress, with heels and hose to boot. Both Cain and Eli had let out low whistles as I came out into the family room to let them know I was taking off.

"Wait a minute," Cain said, narrowing his eyes. "Isn't your date picking you up?"

I rolled my eyes, leaning over to give him a kiss on his cheek. "No, Dad, we're meeting at the restaurant," I replied. "After that debacle with Kenneth, I just couldn't put you guys through that again until I know if he's a keeper."

"Well shit, Paige," Eli piped up. "Don't you even know this dude?"

I leaned over and gave him his kiss, and failed miserably in keeping the smile out of it.

"Yes," I said, rolling my eyes. "I work with him. I told you that. But hell, I didn't think Kenneth would be such a freakin' idiot and I knew him from work as well. If we click, I'll make sure I bring him home for your seals of approval before it gets serious, okay?"

"Well, you definitely look hot, babe," Cain said, his eyes flickering over me from top to bottom. "Shall we expect you home tonight?"

No matter how hard I tried, I couldn't stop the fluttering in my belly whenever Cain got all flirtatious like that with me. It was…unnerving, and yet I enjoyed it.

Eli never seemed to mind it either, which was why I didn't feel badly about the belly flutters he gave me.

"Yes, I'll be home. I quit practicing skankery, or haven't you noticed?"

"We've noticed," they both said at the same time.

"'Kay, then see you guys later."

"Be careful," Cain called out as I hit the door.

I turned back, giving him a smile, watching the intensity that he occasionally threw my way. I think my dating intrigued him for some reason; or maybe it simply bothered him a bit.

"Paige?"

"I'm sorry," I said, coming out of my thoughts to pay attention to my date. "What were you saying, Roger?"

"I said that I have to be totally vigilant when ordering off of menus. I have quite a few food allergies."

"Oh really?" I asked, looking up and over at him. "What kinds?" I figured I might as well know what they were, just in case I invited him over for dinner some time.

"Just some of the more common ones," he replied, giving me a smile. "Fish, including shellfish, poultry meat, nuts, including peanuts, wheat, soy, rice, chocolate and citrus."

Dayumm…

"Well, I'm sure there's something here on the menu that you can tolerate," I replied.

"The thing is," he continued, "I have to make sure that nothing is made *using* peanut oil. You'd be surprised how many different recipes call for peanut oil."

"Really?"

"Oh yeah," he replied, nodding his head. "One time I was at a restaurant in Norfolk, enjoying a dinner salad, when lo and behold, my lips swelled up and my throat started constricting. I was literally gasping for air. It seems that the house dressing was made using peanut oil, unbeknownst to me."

"Damn," I said, "What happened?"

"Well, thank God I had my atomizer with me. I never leave home without it," he replied, tapping the pocket of his jacket. I was okay after a few minutes, but it was a scary few minutes, I can tell you that."

"I can imagine," I replied, glancing down at my menu.

"So even with breads and rolls," he continued, "I have to make sure that they're gluten-free, on account of my wheat allergies."

As dinner droned on, so did the conversation.

But at least Roger had interests in things like sports and music, though he said as a child his allergies to dust, ragweed, and certain types of grasses and trees had made it impossible for him to play outdoor sports.

Roger loved to travel, so he talked about some of the places he'd been. I was genuinely impressed when he told me that he had been to forty-eight of the fifty states.

"So, when are you going to close the loop and hit Alaska and Hawaii?" I asked, as I buttered my dinner roll.

"Not in this lifetime, I'm afraid. I have a fear of flying. So my count stops at forty-eight."

"I see," I nodded.

Roger went on to talk about his job with the bureau, which was actually kind of interesting. He worked for the BAU as a research technician, tracking trends and movements of serial killings.

"You might know my brother," I said. "He's with the BAU, Trace Matthews?"

"Taz?" (My brother's nickname) "Hell yeah, I know him. He's a righteous guy for sure."

Okkaaay.

I could've kissed the waiter as he rolled the dessert cart over to our table to see if we wanted to make a selection. There was a gorgeous crème brulee custard that looked big enough for us to share.

"Can you caramelize the topping?" I asked the waiter.

"I have my trusty kitchen torch right here," he replied with a grin.

"Want to share a crème brulee, Roger?" I asked, arching an eyebrow. I got nothing but a blank stare.

"It's caramel custard," I explained, nodding toward the dessert cart, where the waiter was now torching the top of the sugary topping to make it warm, gooey and crunchy at the same time.

"Oh heavens no," he replied, fanning his face. "You go ahead. I've got a horrible phobia about touching anything sticky," he explained. "I think it goes back to when I was five or six years old, and my twin brother stuck his half-melted caramel apple in my hair at the county fair. My mother damn near scrubbed the hair right off of my scalp."

Dear God. There's another one out there like him?

I turned my attention back to the waiter. "No dessert for us. Check please?"

I insisted on paying for my portion of the dinner bill. I didn't want to give Roger any reason to think that I owed him a good-night kiss, let alone another date—which, by the way, he suggested, and which I politely declined.

I was too embarrassed to return home as early as it was. I didn't want to have to explain to my guys why the hell I was home at nine-thirty from a date that had started at eight.

I stopped at a neighborhood pub that wasn't too far from home and ordered a gin and tonic. I nursed it slowly, killing time until I could head home, making it look as if my second random date hadn't been the complete disaster that it was.

At ten-forty, I paid my tab and headed for home. They had left the front porch light on for me, and I half-expected they'd still be up, even though it was a week night. Cain usually stayed up until midnight. Eli was more regimented in his schedule, being that he got up early for work.

When I came in from the garage, I heard the television going from the family room. I tried to be as quiet as possible, so I could sneak by them without the third degree. I thought I had accomplished just that until I heard Cain's soft voice from behind me.

"How'd it go tonight, Paige?" he asked.

I whirled around to see that it was just him. Eli must've gone to bed.

I walked into the family room, taking my coat off and tossing it over a chair.

"Fortunately, it was nothing memorable," I replied, plopping down next to him on the sofa. "Because, trust me, I'd just as soon gouge both of my eyes out than remember tonight's dating disaster."

"Oh come on," he said, "It couldn't have been as bad as the fiasco with Kenneth, right?"

I gave him an eye roll, and proceeded to fill him in on the fine points of my latest date, complete with the list of Roger's allergies and his phobia of 'sticky things.'

I'd never seen Cain so entertained and amused. Maybe I'd have to continue going on these dating disasters, if only to see his infectious smile and hear his beautiful laughter more often.

"Did Eli go to bed early, or did you just decide to stay up later to make sure I got home safely?" I asked, using my teasing tone with him.

"Yes and yes," he deadpanned. "Want to watch a late flick with me?"

God…yes…

"Hmm," I stalled, glancing up at the clock and seeing it was just a couple of minutes after eleven. "Let me change into my PJ's, and brush my teeth, then I'll hang out with you for a bit. No guarantees I'll stay awake much longer, though. Tomorrow is a work day for me, too."

I went to my room and changed into a pair of flannel pajamas, threw my robe on over them and brushed my teeth. When I returned, Cain had flipped the channel over to one of their subscribed stations, and some terror flick was on.

He had moved down to the end of the sofa.

"Come on," he said, patting the long stretch of sofa next to him. "Stretch out and put your feet in my lap. I'll give you one of my killer foot massages."

Hot damn.

I did as instructed, and within ten minutes, Cain could've asked anything of me and I would've complied.

My God!

This man had some magic fucking fingers that made me glad my feet were nowhere in the vicinity of my pussy, because if they had been, I'd have come about five times by now. He knew every single pressure point and made damn good use of them. I heard myself moan a couple of times, I won't lie; I couldn't help it.

My eyes were closed, but he knew I was still awake.

"So, you're a moaner, are you?"

I opened an eye to look at him.

God, he was so gorgeous when he was intense like that—which was nearly all the time. He hadn't even asked the question in jest. He was dead serious.

"Sometimes," I replied, "If the pleasure is just that good, I mean."

He pulled my feet up and off of his lap, setting them beside him as he moved towards me, his one knee dipped into the cushion on the sofa, his hands supporting his weight rested on either side of me. He hovered over me; his eyes were deadlocked on mine.

"Cain," I started, but never finished whatever it was I'd planned to say, which at the moment, eluded me, because his lips were now brushing against mine, his tongue ever-so-gently tracing my bottom one.

I closed my eyes and went with it, imagining how it would feel to be totally encased by this man. His lips and tongue teased mine almost playfully, but slowly and sensually, as if he were tasting me, centimeter by centimeter.

I raised my arms up and wrapped them around his neck, relishing in the warmth that I could feel with his closeness. Our kiss deepened, and I opened myself up to him, pulling his weight down upon me.

His lips moved slowly to my cheek, planting soft kisses there, his tongue gently lapped at my earlobe. He released a warm sigh against my ear that sent a shiver through me. His tongue traced the outside of my ear, and gently flicked at the edges, as his hands were now framing my rib cage, and moving towards my breasts.

He kneaded my breasts through the double layer of clothing, which still did nothing to repel the heat of his hands on me. His mouth moved to the very sensitive area of my neck, right below my ear, causing me to shiver yet again.

I could tell that he loved making me shiver, and he was an expert at finding other sensitive areas on my neck and throat, taking his time and making soft moans escape from my lips, as his lips and tongue found new ways of pleasuring my skin.

Something in me was responding to him in a way that I'd never done with any other man. For that moment, I didn't care about anything else but melting into him.

My legs struggled beneath him until he raised himself up a bit, so that I could free them up in order to wrap them tightly around his hips.

I pressed myself into him, my legs as strong as a vise in pulling him into me.

I could feel his hardness against my groin as his lips now returned to my mouth, where he found new ways of positioning his lips and tongue, sucking gently on mine as a soft moan now escaped from him.

He thrust his hips gently against me, and mine instinctively rose up to do the same.

Shit…I haven't dry-fucked since eleventh grade.

Cain made no attempt to get underneath my clothing, which was good, because I actually think that no matter how good this felt, I would've stopped him from doing anything skin to skin below my neck.

We struck up a rhythm on the couch. I felt his hardness pressing and grinding against my clit, and that was quickly bringing me to a much-needed orgasm.

Our mouths were melded together, tongues swirling, breathing in one another's breaths. My skin felt flushed with the passionate heat that roiled between us like flames from a fire.

I couldn't stop now. I pressed myself up against him harder, as his hips swiveled against me; his hard cock beneath his jeans rubbed just the right spot, bringing my sweet orgasm to fruition.

I moaned against his lips as I came, trembling from the release that I hadn't had for such a long time, and loving the fact that it was Cain who had given it to me.

In that moment, I didn't feel as if it were wrong. I didn't stop to analyze it, or to even feel guilty about it, because it had nothing to do with anyone other than Cain and me.

Once my orgasm had subsided, I wasn't sure what to do.

I mean, it was kind of a conundrum. I'd gotten mine; he hadn't gotten his and to be honest, there wasn't anything further I was prepared to do to resolve that because of…Eli.

Finally, a bit of shame had sunk in. I moved out from underneath him, not really wanting to talk about it, or anything.

"I need to get to bed, Cain," I said, not really looking at him. I started to get up from the sofa, but he hauled me back down.

"You knew that this was bound to happen, didn't you?"

I was confused. I mean, I'd never *planned* on this happening, and since it had, I was now feeling like it was definitely kind of...*wrong.*

"I never meant for it to," I murmured like a repentant adolescent. "I don't want anything to come between you and Eli."

"It doesn't have to," he replied, taking a lock of my hair, and putting it behind my ear. "It can be about *all* of us."

"What?" I asked; the confusion very evident on my face.

"We have a unique situation," he commented, "But it's not insurmountable, babe. And it's not all that uncommon, given the right circumstances," he finished.

"Are you suggesting...uh," I stammered, looking for the right words.

"A threesome?" he offered.

I nodded my head.

"A threesome is an *event*," he replied. "I'm looking for much more than that, Paige."

"I can't think about any of this now, Cain. It doesn't...feel right to me."

"You go on to bed, and we'll talk about this another time, once you've had a chance to examine your feelings about me...and about Eli."

Eli? Eli couldn't possibly...

"Goodnight," I replied, not wanting to look back at him as I rose from the couch and hurried off to my room.

Much later, I was still lying awake in my room, thoughts and pieces of uncertainty and confusion taking up residence in my brain so that sleep wasn't an option.

From down the hall, I could hear the sounds from their room. I'd heard them before, but tonight it was much more pronounced as the headboard on their bed was rhythmically and loudly banging against the wall of their room.

I guess Cain was getting his after all.

Chapter 13

It was Christmas Eve afternoon and I was trying to get presents wrapped before Cain and Eli arrived home.

They had gone over to Darcy and Easton's for lunch, and I had made an excuse because I knew Trace and Lindsey would be there, and I wasn't all that comfortable being around them. I occasionally ran into Trace in Quantico and it was still strained between us.

I didn't want to think about it. If my brother wanted to blow me off the way that he had, then it was on him, not me.

… And then there was my knitting.

I seriously had turned into some sort of a "knitting Rambo" over the past several weeks, and I really didn't want to blame it on my sexual frustration, because personal denial had actually become one of my strong suits recently - or at least it had until the night after my last dating disaster. Ever since that incident on the couch with Cain, it was like sexual thoughts were coming out of the friggin' woodwork!

I had done my best to avoid being alone with Cain, which wasn't easy because I could feel his brooding eyes on me from the other room.

It was this sexual vibe that had connected us ever since that night that didn't want to be denied. And it was starting to royally piss me off, because Eli had even commented that my knitting creations looked more and more like some sort of phallic symbols.

Pffft!!

They happened to be Christmas stockings for the three of us.

Phallic my ass!

Mine was white with a candy cane embroidered on it, Cain's was red with a gingerbread man on it, and Eli's was green with a snowman on it. I was damn proud of my workmanship. I think my roomies were a bit…puzzled by my newfound domesticity.

They teased me when I baked-six dozen Christmas cookies and a pan of fudge, packing the goodies up in decorative tins to give out to our mail carrier, newspaper delivery person, and our neighbors on either side of us.

Then, between the two of them, they had scarfed down the remaining two dozen cookies, along with the rest of the fudge in a day and a half. After that, Eli practically wouldn't even let me have the T.V. remote because his pants fit tighter two days later.

I had to smile, because I couldn't remember feeling this content or secure, well…ever, I guess.

I no longer missed my random sexcapades, not that those had ever been that fulfilling to begin with. I had even stopped my search for an appropriate boyfriend. I mean who cares if I sat home alone on New Year's Eve? It was seriously over-rated anyway.

My parents had sent me a hefty check for Christmas that I had used to buy the rest of the Christmas presents for

Cain and Eli. Because, quite frankly, I knew the two of them had gone hog wild buying for me.

Yes. I had snooped.

As much as I knew better than to go into their room and dig through their stuff, it had been just too freakin' tempting.

I had justified it by rationalizing that I wasn't going to be outdone in the gift department, despite my poverty-level income. So, yes, I had done what needed to be done in order to make sure that I wasn't totally humiliated on Christmas morning.

Sue me.

I had purchased a pair of black leather gloves for each of them; along with a new Armani tie for Eli and a rechargeable electric wine opener for Cain. I had bought each of them their favorite cologne scents, and with the finished scarves I had knitted, and ear muffs, their Christmas haul was now complete.

As I finished the wrapping, I discovered that I needed one more box for their ear muffs.

Well…shit.

I knew damn well that a box of any size or shape could be found in Eli's closet.

What the hell.

I closed my bedroom door and went into the living room to make sure that they hadn't pulled up yet. Checking up and down the street, twice, I saw it was all clear.

I scurried down the hall to the master suite, opening the door and heading over to Eli's walk-in closet. As I switched the light on, I gasped. There was a shit-load of more Christmas gifts that hadn't been put under the tree yet.

I examined the name-tags, finding four more gifts that had my name on them, which meant that they had done more shopping since my last sweep.

I couldn't resist.

I picked up the first one, shaking it to see if anything jingled. By the size and shape of the box, I was guessing it was some sort of jewelry, but damn - not a sound came from it.

I picked up another one that looked like a box that might have boots in it. I was secretly hoping those were the UGG's I wanted.

I mean, I sure as hell hadn't been crass enough to *ask* for them. But, I *had* left a catalog open on the coffee table in the family room, with the pair that I wanted circled in red for several weeks.

I smiled as I shook the box; pretty damn sure my boots were in there.

Hot damn!

I set the box down and put the smaller one on top, remembering why I had trespassed into forbidden territory to begin with. I searched the shelves over the clothes rack, finally seeing two shoeboxes that would be fine for the two pairs of earmuffs.

I stood on my tip-toes, and moved the bottom box, scooting it toward the edge of the shelf, and jumped back as it fell to the floor, spilling out a pair of Eli's shoes.

As I bent over to pick the shoes up and find a place for them, I heard Cain and Eli come in the front door, none too quietly.

Uh oh…

There was no time to make a quick, unseen exit as I heard their footsteps echoing on the hardwood floors of the hallway.

I quickly switched off the light in the closet, and pulled the louvered door closed; shrinking back into the corner and hoping like hell that Eli didn't need anything out of his closet anytime soon.

Why in the hell hadn't I just gone out when I had the chance? I could have explained the need for a box for a gift way better than if one of them found me hiding in the closet.

"She's probably taking a nap," I heard Eli say as they opened the door and came into their room. "She's been going at all this Christmas stuff with a vengeance," he chuckled. "Just toss those bags on the bed. I'll wrap them later."

"I hear that," Cain remarked. "She's really been on her game, too. She's a hell of a worker, keeps up her end of the bargain, and hell; she even makes this place more of a home for us. Kind of makes me fucking proud of her."

I couldn't see what they were doing, but the discussion they were having immediately piqued my interest.

"I think I know what you're saying, Maddox," Eli replied quietly. "And I want you to know that I'm okay with it."

"I love you, man," Cain murmured. "You and me, we're in this for the long haul, you get that right?"

Eli must've nodded.

"Okay then, so I want you to be *more* than okay with it. I want you to be a *part* of it."

I heard Eli draw a long sigh. I could even picture him doing it.

"I'm not sure I want to cross that line again, Maddox. I mean, I *get* that she's been around with dudes and all, but this is a bit more than even her experience has prepared her for, and she may just end up being a one-dude kind of chick. I mean, the sexually charged current between you two is pretty fucking obvious, but that doesn't necessarily mean she wants *me* to be part of the deal."

Oh God! Are they talking about…what I think they're talking about?

"Eli, this is more than just about sexual chemistry and you damn well know it. This is about a life choice for all of us. I love her same as you, but I need her, too."

"You need to take this slow, Maddox. Yeah, I love her, too. Not the same way that you do, but I think you already knew that. And I love you so fucking much, and your honesty about it all. I won't lose you, I swear. You let her know that you love her, because it's not fair not to. I'm down with whatever it is you need to make this work."

"Come here," Cain ordered quietly.

It was quiet for several moments. I could feel my heart pounding in my chest, and for a second, I was worried that they could hear it too.

I crept quietly over to the door of the closet. The louvers allowed me to see into their room. They were wrapped tightly in an embrace, kissing one another as only people in love kiss.

I watched, curious to see what it was like with these men. I mean, I'd seen them show affection with one another before, but nothing heavy—nothing like right now.

Their lips fit perfectly together as they kissed. Their rock-solid arms were wrapped around one another, and I watched as Eli cupped Cain's chin with his hand, pulling his mouth even closer, allowing his tongue to trace his bottom lip.

Cain kissed Eli the same way that he had kissed me. It was signature. It was custom, I realized, as Cain's hands clasped the back of Eli's neck, pulling him in even further, as if he wanted to devour him. It was almost savage, but it was love, and it was beautiful to me.

Seeing their mutual love expressed so passionately and so fucking willingly to one another, took my breath away.

I decided that I wanted to be kissed like that again. The same way that Cain had kissed me before. I wanted it to happen again. I wanted more to happen because now I was perfectly clear on his feelings. So was Eli.

Cain finally broke away, and I wondered if I was going to see more of their love.

"Come on, Eli," he said, giving him a few more soft, butterfly kisses on his lips, "We'll talk more about this later, for now, we need to get the packages out of the trunk that Darcy sent over and under the tree before Paige wakes up. She gets so excited every time she sees another wrapped package added to the pile."

"Darce sent quite a haul over," Eli replied with a laugh. "I think this is going to be the best Christmas yet."

As soon as I was sure that they had headed back out, I literally came out of the closet, and scurried down the hallway towards my room.

Once inside, I crawled on top of my bed, bringing my legs up to my chin, and rested my head on my knees. I reflected upon the private conversation I'd heard—the one I had no business hearing, even though I was the topic of it. I thought of the way it had made me feel.

I felt warm and giddy inside with the knowledge that I was loved by these men. And I was also humbled by the fact that Eli was sensitive to the fact that with Cain, it was a bit different than it was with him. And he was okay with it. Because that's just how Eli loved.

Chapter 14

Just as I suspected—or should I say, as I was made aware of due to my relentless snooping, I hauled in quite a bit for Christmas. I chastised both Cain and Eli for going overboard.

Eli argued that he had received a nice Christmas bonus at work, while Cain said the catering business had been making major bucks over the holidays, and they had picked up several steady clients for continuing business.

All I knew was that I was officially spoiled this Christmas, and I was a little in love with that.

"My UGG boots," I screeched opening the box and pulling them out. "Oh my God! How'd you guys know?"

That had earned an eye roll from each of them, as I shrugged them on, grinning like a kid who just had their first taste of chocolate.

I also received a leather jacket, a Coach purse, two sweaters, two pairs of jeans, a gold chain necklace, and an assortment of music C.Ds.

Darcy had gifted me with several pairs of earrings, a sweater, hat, gloves and flannel PJs.

Cain rolled his eyes as I pulled out the flannel PJs that had built-in feet. "Those aren't any fun," he teased.

Both of them had loved my gifts to them, totally impressed with my skills at knitting scarves, and they tried them on to show me how they looked.

"You guys have really outdone yourselves," I remarked, looking at my pile of gifts. "This is the best Christmas ever—and it's because of both of you, and the way that I feel about you guys."

It grew quiet as I felt their gazes wrap me up in very secure warmth. I suddenly felt nervous beneath their perusal because they sensed there was more that I wanted to say, and there was.

But I needed to say it to Cain first. And now wasn't the right time. I needed to let him know that, although I loved him—and Eli too for that matter, I wasn't going to be the person who came between them.

We busied ourselves in the kitchen later, getting our Christmas ham in the oven. I watched the way that Eli and Cain interacted and it seemed different—not a bad different, just a subtle quietness that blanketed them and it was new. It was as if a decision had been made; or maybe, a compromise of some sort between the two of them. I was unnerved by it, somehow feeling guilty of something.

I couldn't stop thinking about the conversation I'd overheard and now I wished like hell that I hadn't. And even though they had no clue that I'd heard it, it still hung like a pall over all of us.

Once everything was in the oven, I gathered up all of the boxes containing my Christmas haul, and headed to my room to start putting things in order. Dinner wasn't going to be ready for a couple of hours and I needed some alone time. I sensed they might need some as well.

I'd gotten everything put away in my closet and had made up my bed when there was a light tapping on my door.

"Paige?" It was Cain. "Can I come in?"

"Sure," I called out, plopping down on top of my bed, drawing my knees up under my chin.

He came in, closing my door softly behind him.

"You okay?" he asked, studying me carefully.

"Sure," I said, with faux sincerity. "Why wouldn't I be?"

"No reason. You just seem kind of quiet all of a sudden. Got the Christmas letdown?"

"What's that?" I asked, blinking in confusion.

He smiled. "You know, after the six week build-up and all of the anticipation that goes with it...Then on Christmas, the gifts are opened up and the mystery is gone and it kind of sucks the air out of all that build-up once you realize that it's over for another year."

I smiled weakly. "It's not that. I mean my Christmas was awesome and all. It's something else."

"Wanna share?"

I shifted nervously. "Actually, I was in your room yesterday when you guys got back from Darcy's," I said. "I was looking for boxes to wrap your gifts, and I...kind of panicked when I heard you come home, because I know you don't like me messing with your stuff...so, I uh...hid in the closet," I mumbled, feeling my face flush with embarrassment.

"Go on," Cain urged.

"Okay, so I heard the conversation you had...about me; and how you both feel about...me, and it just sort of seemed...to me that maybe Eli was giving you some kind of permission, you know, to act on it...and, well—I don't know how to feel about that," I finished, finally allowing a sigh to escape.

Cain was still studying me...intently. My admission hadn't seemed to have caught him off-guard, or evoked any major change in his demeanor.

"Paige," he finally said, "You can't pretend that you didn't already know how I've felt about you for a while now. I mean, I think it's been fairly obvious...to the both of us. And I think you reciprocate those feelings, too."

I rested my chin on my knees, and rocked back and forth on the bed slowly. "It doesn't mean that it's right," I whispered. "So, yeah, maybe I have been crushing on you...big time. But you belong to Eli and I know my boundaries these days—I mean, in case you haven't noticed, I'm not the same skank you first met last May, right?"

His face softened; the corners of his mouth curled up into one of his magnificent, though rare, smiles. "I have," he replied, softly. "We both have and we love it. And you're right, baby. I belong to Eli, and he belongs to me,

121

but I want you to belong to me, too. In every sense of the word. And Eli understands that about me and about you. He loves us both, you know?"

I shook my head back and forth. "I know he does," I squeaked, my voice full of emotion. "And it's because I love Eli that I would never feel right about…encroaching. I mean, how in the hell could that ever work, Cain?"

He pulled me from my sitting position, into his strong arms, and I let him. His hand brushed my hair back from my face, and his fingers tilted my chin upward, so that I was forced to look into his beautiful russet eyes.

"We'll just take it slow, baby," he whispered. "Because I have no intention of losing either one of you, got it?"

I didn't have a chance to nod, but I knew that I would have because I had no intention of leaving these men either.

Cain's lips claimed mine with purposeful intent, and I melted into him, responding with my own purpose to claim him right back. My tongue explored him, tasted him, and matched his every movement as my hands fisted through his thick, dark hair, pulling him into me with a hunger I didn't realize existed.

We stayed locked within one another's arms until I felt dizzy with the need for more, and if we didn't stop soon, there would be no stopping. Cain sensed it, too.

He pulled away, cupping my chin and planting, soft kisses on my lips, his eyes smoldering. "We'll take it slow and easy, babe."

I nodded. He pulled away and stood up. I could see that he'd grown hard…for me.

"Eli's leaving in the morning on a ski trip for the next couple of days with some buddies from work. One of them has a condo somewhere in the Shenandoah Valley."

"You aren't going?"

"Have some catering to do. Eli's company shuts down between Christmas and New Year's. I guess it'll just be you and me for the next few days."

I felt myself shiver inwardly, nodding again. And then he was gone. Leaving me there to contemplate what he'd just told me.

Chapter 15

Eli had left for his ski trip before I'd gotten out of bed the following morning. Of course, I'd been awake for a couple of hours. I was just too much of a damned coward to leave my room until I knew that I had the house to myself.

It was Saturday, so I didn't have to report back to work until Monday.

Cain had also left, leaving a note for me on the counter telling me that he'd be back before dinnertime, and making a point of letting me know that we would be having dinner together.

I busied myself doing domestic things, and trying not to think about this evening, when it would be just Cain and me. My stomach butterflies swarmed at the possibilities my imagination was churning out.

Eli hadn't mentioned anything before Christmas about a planned ski trip. This was so not like him. I mean, he'd plan his wardrobe in advance for an excursion such as this to ensure that his ski wear was coordinated perfectly.

This had been a last-minute decision; I knew that now. Eli was giving Cain and me time alone. On purpose.

But why?

Wasn't it obvious?

He loved Cain that much.

Maybe he loved me that much, too.

My heart was racing; jumbled thoughts were running through my head. I didn't think that I'd ever been this nervous—or excited.

I finished up with the house, and then took some steaks out of the freezer for dinner.

I took a leisurely bath, shaving, waxing and buffing my skin to a healthy glow.

I painted my nails, and selected some sexy new underwear that I had purchased as a Christmas gift to myself. I dressed in a pair of my new skinny jeans and one of the sweaters I'd received from Eli and Cain.

I brushed out my damp hair, blowing it dry and straightening it with my flat iron. Once I had applied a bit of bronzer and eye make-up, I studied my reflection in the mirror.

I knew what was going to happen this evening and for now, I was okay with that, because I knew in my heart, that it was what I wanted and what I needed.

∞∞∞∞∞∞∞∞∞∞∞∞∞∞∞∞∞∞∞∞∞∞∞∞∞∞∞∞∞∞

I was in the kitchen, marinating the steaks and putting a salad together when Cain got home. It was damn near seven o'clock and I could tell that it had been a day for him. He came up behind me and my skin immediately goose-bumped hard.

"I was going to take you out," he said to me softly, his breath warm on the back of my neck. "Today's event was one disaster after another, it seems. I meant to call you before I realized how late it was. Sorry, baby."

"It's fine," I said, not daring to look at him while I continued chopping celery for the salad. "Let's stay in and have a quiet dinner."

"I'm gonna grab a quick shower, then I'll be out to help you, I promise."

"No, Cain. You worked today. I've got this, okay?"

He put his arms around me, and kissed the top of my head gently. "I won't be long," he said with a promise in his voice.

I shivered.

Dinner was quiet and intimate. The two glasses of wine I consumed had taken the edge off, and maybe had even served to give me some courage. We needed to deal with the elephant in the room before anything else progressed.

"So, have you talked to Eli today?" I asked, looking up from my plate.

"No," he answered quietly. "I don't expect to hear from him while he's away. He needs this time for himself."

"Cain," I started, but he quickly interrupted.

"It was his idea, Paige. Totally. He wants this for us and if I wasn't absolutely sure of that, I'd be with him at Massanutten right now. Do you understand that?"

"But—"

"It's what he wants, Paige. It's what I want and you fucking know that it's what you want," he said firmly, his eyes now flickering over me with an expression that left no doubt in my mind that he was right.

"What is it that you think I want?" I challenged, because I had to hear it from his lips.

"You want to know what it feels like when my cock is buried deeply inside of you, after my tongue has tasted every fucking bit of you first," he said, huskily. "You want to know that, when I'm inside of you that it's just me and you—and no one else, and that each and every time I thrust my cock into you—that it's for you and you alone, and when I finally come—it's because of you and what you do to me that made that happen—and that it's all yours and only yours."

My God.

My panties were damp because of his words; I felt my tongue sweep across my upper lip as I finally exhaled a breath I hadn't known I'd been holding.

"That's just fucking," I finally said, looking at him and tilting my chin up just a bit.

I saw a glint in his eye as he knew I wanted more.

"Oh yeah," he breathed, sipping his wine. "We're going to fuck for sure. And then we're going to make love, and then maybe fuck again before we finally sleep. Do you have a problem with that?"

"No," I whispered, my limbs turning to jelly right where I sat.

"Good," he said, "Because tomorrow is Sunday and we're both going to be resting up so that we can do it all again afterwards...and again."

Cain got to his feet, and circled around to where I was sitting. He pulled my chair out for me, and he extended his hand down to me. I placed my hand in his, and he pulled me up to my feet where I stood before him.

His hand went to my face; he tilted my chin up to look into the depths of his eyes.

"Are you sure?" he asked, his voice every bit as intense as his eyes.

I nodded, keeping eye contact with him, making sure that he could read the message very clearly in my eyes: I was never surer of anything in my life.

"For the first time ever, I feel like I belong somewhere...with someone...with you," I breathed.

And what he did next, I'll never forget.

He gathered me up into his strong arms, and I immediately laced my arms around his neck.

"You're mine" he said huskily, as he carried me down the hallway towards the master suite.

I'm pretty sure everything in my body just...stopped what it was doing, so that my pulse, heartbeat and shallow breathing could just pay attention to what was currently happening.

He lowered me down to my feet once we were there; his arms now drew me up against him. Standing there for a minute that felt like two seconds in this man's arms, I felt his lips breeze across my forehead. He tilted my face upward to his, and sought my lips with his own as I melted against him.

I was dizzy with his nearness, his breath warm against my throat as he whispered against me. "God, you're so sweet, Paige. So fucking sweet."

My arms laced around his neck, my face was buried against his chest. I felt his heartbeat and it was strong, and steady. His fingers traced the sensitive skin at the nape of my neck, and he gently fisted my hair, drawing my face back as his mouth now came crashing down on mine with clear purpose and intent.

His lips worked mine expertly, and I moaned with the pleasure of feeling his tongue exploring my mouth, capturing my bottom lip in a soft suck, and then tracing his tongue over my top lip, nipping gently at it. I felt heady with his taste and his scent.

His hands moved to my torso, where he pulled my sweater up and over my head, his hands eagerly moving to unclasp my bra so that he could access my breasts, fondling them with urgency, fingering my nipples and causing me to shiver against him.

I felt him unbutton my jeans, and I assisted, getting them lowered to my feet so that I could step out of them. And just like that, he'd discarded his clothing and his eyes took in every inch of my naked body. Mine did the same and he was magnificent. Just like I knew that he would be.

He was back to me, capturing my lips once again, as he lifted me up against him, and then gently lowered me down onto their bed.

There was nothing gentle about his kisses at the moment. The sheer intensity of that was mind-fucking-boggling, as he consumed my lips with his, and claimed my tongue. I felt his hardness against me and my body ached to feel all of him.

I thrust my hips up against him as he roughly fondled my breasts with his large, strong hands, before dipping his head lower, and pulling one into his mouth, nursing it as if it had always been his and no one else's.

I moaned in pure pleasure as I felt his teeth, nipping at my flesh, drawing my nipple in deeper, and then rolling it with his tongue until I thought I would come from that alone.

He moved to the other one, possessing it with his mouth and tongue, and I felt my legs wrap around his hips, drawing him closer, as if that were even possible.

"I need you inside of me," I moaned softly, my hand now fisting in his thick, dark hair. "Please, baby?" I whimpered.

"Patience, babe," his lips said against my sensitive skin, as he moved himself lower.

His tongue was now blazing a slow, sensuous trail down my belly, while his hands moved even lower; and his fingers gently plied the folds of my pussy apart. I felt myself rock against him as he inserted one finger, and then another into my sanctum, gently probing the depths as my wetness coated them.

His tongue flickered over my slit, lapping each sensitive fold of my pussy, and then plunged inside of my core, where it joined his fingers, as the heat of his touch slowly enveloped my senses into this moment in time. I never wanted this feeling to end.

I moaned audibly, thrusting my pelvis up against him, swiveling my hips so that every nerve ending in my core was being touched by him.

He continued loving my pussy, moaning to himself as he tasted my wetness and his tongue washed over my clit again and again, sending shock waves through me from head to toe.

He felt my trembling, knowing already that I was very near climax, so he slowed his tempo a bit, rising up from me to reach for the condom on the nightstand next to the bed.

All the while, his fingers continued their gentle probing of my sex, as he effectively removed the condom from the wrapper and rolled it onto his rigid cock with one hand.

He was on his knees, his eyes boring into me with a hungry passion that owned me.

"I want to fuck you this way," he said, grabbing a pillow and raising my hips up so that he could position it underneath my ass. "I want to watch you come with my cock inside of you."

I nodded.

All that I could think about was that, at this moment, Cain was mine. He was all about me. I didn't have to share. Every kiss, every thrust, every lick was for me and only me.

He grabbed my legs, and positioned them over his shoulders, leaning in as his hand guided his sheathed cock into me with a forceful thrust.

I moaned in pleasure, licking my lips as I watched his muscular thighs; he knelt between my raised legs, and rocked in and out of me with slow deliberation.

I was mesmerized by him in every way. He tilted his head back, closed his eyes and totally focused on his thrusting, his hands now cupping my ass, lifting me up just a bit and adjusting me for his fit.

His cock was teasing my G-spot, and that's when I felt my body take over; my muscles tightened around his girth; and I heard his sharp intake of breath as they did.

"Christ baby," he rasped, his eyes now coming open in surprise. "You're going to milk my cock, aren't you?"

"Uh huh," I murmured, feeling myself contract once again around his swollen member.

"Because this is mine, Cain," I whispered. "This is for me. I want you to fuck me like you mean it."

"Aww…baby," he breathed, watching me as I was slowly being wrecked by this man, "You know I mean it," he replied, driving himself even deeper into my heat.

Our tempo increased and, together, we spiraled into a perfect orgasm, our eyes deadlocked and my mind totally obliterated with the things that he made me feel, physically and emotionally.

Fuck.

I loved him.

Totally.

Chapter 16

I learned quickly that Cain had not exaggerated one bit when he laid out our agenda for the weekend. We had alternated between fucking and making love all through the night.

I had never known just how totally electrifying having a man's cock buried inside of me could be until it was Cain's. I had moaned and mewled those feminine sounds at the pleasure he gave me, but for once they were real—not fake the way I had done so many times before. Because this was real and it totally rocked. Cain had made me his and I wasn't going anywhere. I knew that there was no way I could ever walk away from this—from him.

I was still curled up in his arms, naked and totally satiated from the night. His slow, even breathing against the back of my neck soothed me and made me feel so fucking secure that I never wanted to leave this bed.

But I knew that it wasn't possible. Because this was still *their* bed. And the guilt momentarily washed over me, so I gently moved Cain's arm from around my torso, and scooted towards the edge of the bed.

"Where are you going?" his husky voice asked from behind me.

"I...uh...I thought maybe a shower?" I said, putting it more like a question than a statement.

"We can do that," he said, rousting himself up. "But we're doing it together."

And that's exactly how our Sunday went. We did everything together.

We showered, we ate, we made love, we watched television, we ate, we fucked, we showered again and then we cuddled and I was thinking that cuddling with my man was pretty fucking awesome too.

I put the flannel PJ's with the feet in them that Darcy had given me for Christmas on after our last shower. I returned to the bathroom, dressed, to hang up my damp towels.

Cain was standing in front of the mirrored vanity, towel slung low on his hips shaving when he happened to glance over at me and then did a double take.

"Ah, hell to the no, woman," he barked, his brow cocked; a hint of amusement flickered across his face.

"What?" I asked innocently, looking down at my totally-covered-in-flannel body.

"You'll not be wearing that shit to bed because I swear I'll rip them off of you. Unacceptable, babe."

"Cain," I whined, "For Chrissake, I'm sore. Can we just cuddle for a bit?"

He turned back to the mirror, tilted his face upward so that he could take his razor up under his chin.

"We did that cuddling shit earlier," he replied, shaking the razor to get the shaving cream off in the sink full of water. "This is our last night together," he said plainly. "I want to make it memorable."

I had to smile. "On two conditions," I parried.

He looked at my reflection in the mirror, quirking a brow again and waiting to hear my conditions.

"First," I said, "We sleep in my room tonight, okay?"

He nodded and waited for me to continue.

"Secondly, uh…can you be extra gentle?" I asked hesitantly because, the truth was, my crotch was, in fact, sore from all the attention he'd been giving it for the last day and a half.

"Why do you think I'm standing here removing my face stubble, babe? You think I can't see your reddened skin?"

I felt myself blush, of all things. Where in the hell did that come from? This man had seen and licked every inch of my body, including every crack and crevice, the truth be told.

I stifled a giggle and left the bathroom, pulling off all of the sheets on their bed and throwing them into the washer.

I re-made their bed with fresh sheets and blankets.

"Why are you doing that?" Cain asked as he came out of the bathroom, wearing a white T-shirt and low-slung pajama pants.

I shrugged. "I just don't think I want Eli to come home to sheets that…you know?"

"What? Smell like our sex?"

"Yes," I said, quickly, tossing a bit of a glare into it.

"Don't you think that I would've had the good sense to do that?" he asked.

"I'm sorry, Cain," I sighed. "This is just…new to me. I don't think I'll know how to act around him when he comes home."

I was tucking in the top sheet when he came over and pulled me around to face him.

"Stop," he said firmly. "Eli knows what's happening with us this weekend and he is fine with it," he said, annunciating the last six words.

I turned from him, and continued making up the bed. "He's *fine* with it because he loves *you*," I said, a hint of exasperation in my voice. "And he would allow this before he'd ever want to lose *you* and I guess I don't blame him."

"Hey," he said, a little louder, "He loves you, too. He doesn't want to lose *you* either."

"It's not the same, Cain," I said, sighing loudly. "It's just not the same thing."

He grabbed me then, pulling me up against his hard chest. "You need to give it some time, baby. You'll see. It's all gonna work out fine."

He stroked my hair with his hand, and he held me against him and for a minute, I wanted to totally believe that he was right.

That everything would work out fine.

Chapter 17

To say that things were a bit…strange after Eli returned home Monday evening would be a bit of an understatement.

I mean, Cain was fine. It was as if nothing had changed between him and Eli, but I couldn't say the same for me.

All kinds of fucked-up emotions were springing forth, ranging from guilt and shame, to a little bit of resentment when they headed off to their room that night…together, as in at the *same time*, which almost never happened.

I went to bed with my ear buds in, listening to a heavy metal station because I'd be damned if I was going to let myself get lulled to sleep by the sound of their headboard banging a tune against their wall. And that's when the resentment part really started seeping in, and I know that's fucked up, alright?

I busied myself at work, and then stayed late to work out each night at the gym so that I would miss dinner with my guys. It seemed that putting up with Darin's little comments and innuendos in the weight room was preferable to my feeling like some twisted bitch home-wrecker.

The truth was that Eli hadn't been anything but sweet to me since his return home. Yet something had changed and we both knew it.

I would lie alone in my bed every night and feel totally clueless as to how I was supposed to handle this. I ached for Cain, but I knew that I really had no right to feel that way, if that made sense.

It was Thursday and it was New Year's Eve to boot. Long holiday weekend.

Fucking lovely.

I was just finishing up with my filing when my cell rang. It was Cain.

"You gonna be home for dinner tonight or are you going to continue avoiding me?"

I took a moment to gather my thoughts because he was right. I no longer felt comfortable around him—or Eli for that matter. This was too difficult for me. I didn't possess the emotional armor to be able to pull something off like this. At all.

"I'm sorry," I squeaked out. "You're right—I have been avoiding you guys."

"Why?" he deadpanned, as if it weren't totally obvious.

"I don't care who's blessing we have, Cain. I can't do this. I just can't. I love Eli too much. There. I've said it."

"What the fuck? You think that Eli and I don't love you every bit as much?"

"First off, Cain, I don't think that *you* should be the one speaking for Eli, okay? And secondly—regardless of how we all love one another, I can't share. Period. I'm going to find another place to live."

"The hell you are," he growled at me. "You're not going anywhere, Paige. You need to face the facts *right* here and right now."

"Oh no," I said, tossing some downright haughtiness into my voice. I swiveled around in my desk chair so I faced the wall, hoping my voice didn't carry.

"You don't *get* to tell me what I can and cannot do. It's clear to me that you've not gone without fucking…*someone* since Eli came home. And how fucking pathetic is it that I *even* just said that to you? Jesus Christ, this is *so* not who I want to be," I halfway wailed. "So, to answer your question? I won't be home for dinner tonight…or breakfast tomorrow. Happy fucking New Year."

End Call.

Chapter 18

I managed to find somewhere to crash for the night so that I could have some time to think things through like I needed to. One of my co-workers, Julie, came by as I was sitting in my car in the parking lot, staring into space and totally clueless as to where I could go.

"Hey, Paige," she called out, tapping on my car window. "Are you okay?"

The thing was, I didn't have girl friends, or sisters or even a brother that I felt comfortable confiding in when something like this was tearing me apart. All I had were Eli and Cain, and they were the problem.

I lowered my window. "Just some drama with roommates," I replied. "I suddenly wish it weren't a long, holiday weekend."

"You want to crash at my place?" she offered.

It was tempting, but I sure as hell didn't want her trying to dig into the details of my roommate problems in an effort to give me some sage advice.

"I mean, I'm staying with Rick over the New Year holiday so it's like you'd have the place to yourself...well almost, that is," she laughed. "Can you feed my cat, Brutus?"

Done fucking deal.

And so that's how it went.

I went to Julie's and spent the night, talking to Brutus and spilling my guts to him about my issues with these men. He was a great listener (for a tabby cat) and the best thing was that he never got judgy with me.

We rang in the New Year together. He just purred and rubbed against my ankles for most of the night, making sure that he had put his scent on me, like any other normal male I suppose.

I knew that Cain had a New Year's Day banquet to cater, and I'd heard Eli on the phone making plans to go to Darcy's for the traditional New Year's Day feast. He'd even invited me to go with him, but I had begged off, not looking him in the eye because he knew me well enough to know if I were lying.

Not that I lied to either one of them...anymore.

I left to return home at one o'clock, fairly certain that they'd both be out.

And then what?

I got on my cell and did the only thing that I could do under these circumstances.

"Hey Trace," I said when he picked up. "Happy New Year."

<u>Chapter 19</u>

What a great way to start off the New Year! (Said no one ever.) I groveled to my older brother, who hadn't really been speaking much to me since I'd been tossed out of their home for having cunnilingus on their kitchen countertop. I now had the ultimate pleasure of asking him for temporary refuge, explaining that I would fill him in on the details later.

I'd have to create some plausible reason other than the truth, or I'd be tossed out once again, I was sure.

I obviously couldn't ask Easton because of Darcy's close relationship with Eli. She'd have it all figured out in a nanosecond.

I mean, hopefully my application for a full-time position with the F.B.I. would be approved and I'd receive a salary that could sustain my livelihood, but I was fully prepared that, if that didn't happen, then maybe it was just a sign that it was time for me to move on.

I pulled into our driveway and breathed a sigh of relief. Cain's car was gone, and as soon as I hit the remote for the garage, I saw that Eli's was gone as well.

I grabbed several empty boxes from the garage and headed into the house with them. I was determined to work quickly and efficiently to clear out my closet and dresser drawers before either of them returned. I figured I had a couple of hours, minimum.

I emptied my closet and took those boxes out and put them in the trunk of my car. I grabbed a couple of more empty ones and headed back to pack up my dresser drawers.

I was just finishing up when I heard the slam of the front door, and footsteps coming down the hall.

Fuck.

My bedroom door was open, which was probably fortunate, because I would've hated to see the damage done had it been closed and locked.

Eli came in, his light blue eyes flashing with something akin to anger mixed with pain.

"So, this is what you're about?" he growled, his hands on his hips, glaring at me.

"Wh-What?" I croaked in confusion. "How did—?"

"How did I know?" he asked, eyes flashing. "You forget that Lindsey and Darcy talk almost hourly. She shared with Darce that you were to be a temporary houseguest. Wasn't all that hard to figure out you were bailing on us."

I shook my head, looking down at the floor.

Stupid! Stupid! Stupid!

"Answer my question, Paige. You were just gonna leave *us* like that?"

"Eli," I said with a sigh, sitting down on my bed. "Calm down, okay? This is for the best. I can't even look at you because...of..."

"Of what?" he growled, flexing his hands at his sides as if he wanted to punch something...or someone.

Fuck. He's furious.

"Because of what I did...with Cain. And don't you dare tell me that you're fine with it because I don't fucking believe that."

He grabbed me by the arm, pulling me roughly to my feet. I was standing within inches of him, and I could feel the heat of his anger envelope me.

"You *love* Maddox," he said, his words very distinct. "And you love me, too. You think I don't know that?"

"I know that you do, but it's different."

"Hell yeah, it's different," he growled. "I fucking love you, Paige, and yeah, it's different than the way that I love Maddox, but that doesn't make it inconsequential now, does it?"

His hands were locked around my wrists, forcing me to look at him.

"I don't understand," I replied, honestly.

"Baby," he sighed. "You are trying to compartmentalize this situation. It's not black and white; it's not right or wrong. It's not *even* fifty-fifty because everyone's different, just as everyone's needs are different."

He relaxed his grip on me a bit, and pulled me down next to him as he sat down on my bed.

"I knew from the time that I was in junior high school that I was attracted to both sexes, but it's not like you think—like most people think. I'm attracted to the individual first; the gender is secondary to that. People automatically assume that bisexuals are simply people who want both genders sexually and cannot be monogamous to either. That's just not true."

"So then why did Cain refer to you as being a 'closet' bisexual? I mean, that suggests that you have an overall preference...to the male gender."

He nodded his head, and clasped his hands together under his chin, taking a moment.

"I'm not sure what all Maddox told you," he said, and I realized I probably shouldn't have blurted out what I had. "But the truth is that I fell in love with an exchange student from Sweden my senior year of high school. Her name was Greta. I'd prefer not going into the details with you right now, but suffice it to say, I was in love with her. She hurt me deeply, and after that, I made a conscious choice to focus on the male gender only for future relationships. It worked out well until I met...Darcy."

What?

"What?" I gasped. I felt my eyes widen in surprise.

He nodded, his eyes caressing my face and I could tell this just might be the first time that he'd shared this with anyone.

"It's true," he said, wistfully. "I didn't set out for that to happen, but I kinda fell in love with her. And, I mean, it was the hardest thing that I've ever had to control," he said with a laugh. "But, control it I did because the simple truth was that I had no faith in my ability to sustain a relationship with a female...after Greta, that is."

"But Eli," I said, taking his hand, "You mean that Darcy never knew?"

"That's right," he said, "Oh hell, I knew the morning after she'd first slept with Easton that she was gone. And that was fine because the beautiful thing was that I had met Maddox that same night. I knew that Darce would always be in my life, and I'm satisfied with that. Just like I know that Maddox will always be in my life. But you," he said solemnly, "You, I'm not sure of and I don't want to lose you because of *my* fear that I can't sustain a relationship with another female...after Greta."

I swallowed nervously. This was all new information for me. I never suspected that Eli had been drawn to me in that way...at all. I just knew that, at this moment in time, he had opened himself up to me in a way that even Cain had never done, and that made me love him so much differently.

"Oh my God," I breathed, turning to face him. "All of this time, I've loved you because I saw how much you loved Cain. So much, that you were willing to share him with me because of that love for him. And... you know, Cain tried to tell me that it was different than that, but I swear to God, Eli, you've never acted on...any sort of attraction towards me, I mean..."

He interrupted, pulling me closer to him on the bed. "Baby," he said softly. "It's because I see that chemistry going back and forth between you and Maddox…and, I guess I'm just not sure if there's enough of that same chemistry—in you—left over for me. Because I know that there's plenty in me left for you—if you want it, I mean."

And I think he might've just blushed right then, like a guy that was wearing his heart on his sleeve—just putting it right out there and so worried that it might not be enough.

But it was enough.

It was more than enough.

"Oh Eli," I sighed, "I can't believe you've told me all of this, but I am so fucking glad that you have."

Our eyes met and locked. In that moment, everything that Cain had assured me of since we'd given in to our feelings was coming true.

I leaned over and brushed my lips softly against his, waiting for him to snake his arms around me and pull me against to him.

I didn't wait long until that was exactly what he did.

We kissed and it was unfamiliar, but it was sweet. And every second, it became sweeter. I felt myself warm to his touch; my belly tingled with anticipation of where he might touch me next and I wanted him to touch me in different places.

He turned and pulled me into his lap, his fingers tilted my chin back so that his eyes could study mine and I saw the warmth fill them.

"God, baby. We're going to do this."

He lifted me up into his strong arms, carried me to their room, and gently deposited me on their bed. The same bed that I had shared with Cain, I was now going to share with Eli and I wanted it. I wanted it more than I thought I ever could.

"Get undressed," he ordered, "We'll do the sensual shit another time, but for right this second, I need to be inside of you and claim you as mine, too."

God, his words made me wet and yeah, that surprised the hell out of me as well. I scrambled to do as he ordered, shedding my clothes quickly; leaving my thong on so that he would be the one to relieve me of it when it was time...

He was standing there naked and he was every bit as beautiful as Cain. His body was well-muscled and his belly flat. He had a lighter complexion than Cain, but God he was beautiful in a "golden-boy" sort of way. I felt myself getting wet just in anticipation of what would happen next.

He opened the bedside table drawer, and pulled out a handful of condoms.

Holy shit.

He pushed me back against the pillows on the bed, his eyes taking in all of my nakedness with a hunger. He straddled me with his strong, muscular thighs, leaning forward to capture my lips with his.

I laced my arms around his strong neck, pulling him in closer. I felt his fingertips lightly caressing my breasts, slowly and methodically tugging at my nipples until they grew hard for him. He moved his mouth to one, his tongue circling the soft peaks, and his fingers gently kneading my breast so that he could begin suckling.

I drew in a sharp breath as he took the nipple into his mouth and sucked hard on it, my pussy now fairly soaked in anticipation. I needed him inside of me every bit as much as he wanted to be there.

I rolled to my side so that I could feel his warmth, my tongue tracing his lips as he moved his mouth back up to mine, and pulled me against his nakedness.

Damn.

And suddenly, there were another pair of hands in the mix. I hadn't heard Cain come in, but he was there and he was intent upon joining us.

I felt his calloused fingertips gently rubbing my lower back and smoothing over my hips, where his thumbs hooked into the elastic band of my thong, and he slowly lowered it down, where it pooled around my feet on the bed.

Eli's mouth moved from mine, and I watched as Cain, already stripped down to his tee shirt and boxers, leaned in and captured Eli's lips with his, their tongues swirling together in a frenzied and familiar passion.

I watched, totally mesmerized by their rhythm and cadence, caught between them, and feeling the heat of their love wrapped around me like a cozy blanket.

I felt Eli lift me from the bed, my feet shrugged out of the thong that had pooled there, and I gazed at Cain as he quickly discarded his tee shirt and bottoms.

His cock sprang free; it was thick and bold, as it slapped against his abdomen. His eyes were hooded with lust, but he was in and that made me so fucking happy.

He leaned over and his tongue traced the outside of my lips. "I need to taste you again, Paige."

Sweet Jesus.

I wanted him—I wanted both of them—to do anything and everything that they desired.

He smiled, and nodded to Eli, who was standing beside the bed now, totally hard. Cain reclined back on the bed, shifting himself so that he was on his back in the middle. I watched as his hand gripped his cock, stroking it up and down a few times, which made me want to slide my pussy over it.

They had something else in mind.

I felt Eli wrap his strong arms around my waist, and lift me so that I was directly over Cain's face.

"Spread your legs apart, baby," he instructed, as he gently lowered me so that my thighs were now framed on either side of Cain's head.

I felt Cain's hands brace the back of each thigh, as I straddled him. I leaned forward, and rested my weight onto each of my elbows, tilting my ass upward as his warm mouth met the wetness of my pussy.

Eli took his place at the end of the bed, parting Cain's thighs, and wrapping his hand around Cain's rigid cock, running it up and down with firm stroking.

I was dizzy with pleasure as I felt Cain's tongue run up and down my slit, licking and lapping my juices as I moaned and shuddered.

His fingers plied apart the soft folds, swirling his tongue around and around each one; gently nipping until I thought I would scream, and then plunging his tongue in and out of my core. My hips were swiveling to meet his thrusting tongue as he totally fucked me with his mouth.

"Oh God," I whimpered as I felt myself dissolving into him.

My eyes were locked on Eli, watching as he leaned over, and took Cain's cock into his mouth, his other hand now stroking his own very impressive erection. Eli's blue eyes were locked on me, and in that moment, it felt like we had reached the same peak of pleasure and had somehow shared it.

"You ready to come, baby?"

The words that Cain spoke against the lips of my pussy took me to the edge.

"That's it baby," he said softly against me, "Just let it happen. I need to taste it."

Oh...God!

His tongue plunged into my depths as my orgasm released around me; my muscles clenched as I moaned, unable to hold the release back one more second, not that I wanted to. I heard him moan against me as Eli brought him to climax with his mouth, the sound of wet sucking and the feel of Cain pumping against Eli's mouth made my orgasm electrifying.

I moaned and shuddered as the last of it wound down, my heart beating so fast I could barely catch my breath.

Cain suddenly clenched his jaw; his body became rigid as he emptied his climax into Eli's mouth. They both moaned in manly pleasure which totally, fucking rocked.

Afterwards, when I felt as if I could move again, I pulled my legs up and over and fell on my back next to Cain. His hand moved to my head, turning my face towards his and his lips and tongue found mine, kissing me sweetly and softly, moving his tongue inside of my mouth so that I could taste my orgasm.

Eli stretched out on the other side of me, his erection bold against my backside, his lips tracing a pattern on the back of my neck as I continued kissing Cain.

"My turn," he whispered huskily, pulling me against him, his hands now gently massaging my breasts.

"You ready to share, Maddox?" he asked, a hint of pure amusement and lots of happiness now evident in his voice.

"No, but I will," Cain said, as his lips moved from mine. "Let's see what you can do."

Cain moved aside, grabbing two condoms from their nightstand drawer, along with some lube.

Two?

He tossed a condom to Eli, who quickly ripped open the foil packet, and rolled it onto his thick and very-erect shaft.

Eli was on his knees now, hovering above me, but only for a moment, before he leaned in and captured my mouth with his. I wrapped my arms around his strong neck, bringing him in closer, wanting to taste him once again. Because he was mine, too.

I felt his fingers gently massaging the soft peaks of my breasts, twirling a nipple between his thumb and index finger, giving it a gentle pinch. His mouth moved downward, sucking the soft mounds; and his tongue teased the rosy peaks as my back arched upward, wanting to feel his bold erection against my slit.

"Somebody's greedy, Maddox," he said, and I caught a glimpse of Cain, hovering behind Eli, stroking his own sheathed cock which was fully erect once again.

I watched in total fascination as Cain rubbed lube onto his shaft, and then onto his fingers. His hands moved out of sight, but I could tell by Eli's sharp intake of breath where they had gone.

"Are you ready for me, baby?" Eli asked, his eyes hooded with pleasure as Cain continued to stroke him from behind.

"Yes, Eli," I whispered, gazing up into his pale blue eyes.

He shifted his position a bit, arching his back so that his ass tilted upward a bit to allow Cain access; while he guided his very erect cock into my pussy with a slow and deliberate thrust.

"Mmm," I moaned, feeling his fullness inside of me.

I wrapped my legs around his torso, my feet locked together as Eli began to rock in and out of me.

He paused momentarily, and I could tell that Cain had entered him from behind, but my vision was blocked by Eli's body, moving in and out of me.

"Fuck," he growled. "Maddox, take it slower or I'm gonna lose it right now and I need to feel more of her pussy. Been a while, dude."

I heard a soft chuckle from Cain, but Eli was intent on fucking me and I was glad because I needed to feel him and know that it was him and that I loved him, too.

"That's it," I breathed as he pumped into me again and again.

"God Paige, your pussy is squeezing my dick like a mother-fucker," he rasped. I could once again feel his rhythm change as Cain was thrusting into him.

The cadence of our fucking had changed and the only way I could describe it was that it was truly a team effort. Cain rocked into Eli, who rocked into me, and I bucked my hips back in the same rhythm, which was quickly causing a sexual frenzy for all of us.

Eli ravaged my lips with his as the pleasure elevated into a crescendo of raw passion and fury.

"Oh God," I moaned as I felt my muscles constrict around him, my core had a pulse as the contractions milked him fluidly.

"Fuucck," he growled loudly, as his cock throbbed like a heartbeat and his climax emptied inside of me.

From somewhere in the sensual fog of our orgasms, I heard Cain moan deeply, and felt Eli shudder as our trifecta was brought perfectly to fruition.

I had never felt anything quite as intense or as magical as what I'd just felt with these men.

And it totally rocked.

Chapter 20

(Cain)

I awoke realizing that I was all tangled up in Eli, which wasn't all that unusual, but I could've fucking sworn that Paige had fallen asleep between us last night. We'd all fallen asleep tangled up in one another's limbs, butt naked and exhausted but fulfilled—all of us. That much I knew for certain.

I've got to say that I was fucking surprised when I'd walked into our room yesterday afternoon and saw what was starting to happen with Eli and Paige. I was not only surprised, I was pleased as fuck. It had been a tough week for all of us, but my instincts had been right.

I hadn't been sure just how comfortable my partner was going to be taking a walk back over to the other side. I mean, hell, it wasn't as if he hadn't been there plenty of times before, but something about his high school romance, and brief marriage to Greta, an exchange student from Sweden, that he'd knocked up during their senior year in high school, had changed all of that.

It wasn't as if Greta had even been his first.

Hell, he'd shared with our counselor that he'd fucked the whole varsity cheer squad during his junior year in high school; a couple of them at the same time he'd even bragged.

But Eli came from good people. He and his brothers were cowboys for Chrissake—growing up on a horse ranch in Wyoming. The only difference between Eli and his brothers was that Eli's boots had to be designer. That was just how my man rolled.

He had told me that, even in junior high school, he'd been attracted to both sexes, but he'd decided he was only going to pursue chicks. And pursue he had.

But when Greta got knocked up, the dude wanted to do the right thing, and he said at that point, he knew any desires he had for the male gender had to be retired permanently, because he planned on making a life with her and their kid.

So, both of them being eighteen years of age had taken off to find a JP and they had eloped.

Of course, as soon as Greta's sponsor, Youth for Understanding, found out about the situation, her knocked-up ass was put on a plane back to Sweden. It was something about her violating the terms of her student visa, and she was put on home country restriction, meaning she couldn't apply for a U.S. residency visa for another two years.

I guess Eli had e-mailed her like crazy, but her e-mail account had been closed. He tried writing to her as well, but the letters were returned to him unopened.

The marriage was annulled and he had never heard a thing from her again. It bugged him, knowing that somewhere on the planet, he had a kid that he'd never see or know. He had some trust issues after that where females were concerned.

But last night, it was apparent that Paige and Eli were down with each other. Like nothing I'd ever fucking imagined. It'd been pretty intense, but intense was good, right? I was just bothered by the fact that she'd left our bed sometime during the night.

I was worried that she was having second thoughts, and I knew that I couldn't handle losing her, especially since she was under my skin to stay.

I quietly extricated myself from Eli and grabbed my boxers from the floor, shrugging them on.

I went to her room and fuck if the door wasn't shut. That didn't stop me from opening it and letting myself in. Her bed was empty, but she'd slept in it, I could tell.

"What? You don't knock?" I heard her ask, coming out of her bathroom wearing a towel around her body, and her hair wrapped in another. She was sporting a sexy little grin, so I knew that she wasn't really pissed at me.

"Why knock?" I asked her with a shrug. "I've memorized every inch of your body, so there's really nothing to hide from me, is there?" I didn't give her a chance to respond. "What I'd like to know is *why* you're in here instead of with us in our room."

She turned from me and walked the few feet over to her dresser, grabbing a comb from it. "I just wanted to take a shower, that's all," she replied.

"Looks like you did more than that," I said, nodding towards her unmade bed as she turned to face me.

"Do we need to get a bigger bed in our room? Or is it something else?"

I felt myself tense up because, at that moment, I wasn't reading her…at all.

My throat constricted because, fuck, I didn't know what I'd do if she said this arrangement was not for her.

She sat down on her bed, and removed the towel from her hair, rubbing sections of her long, damp locks with it. Her brown eyes met mine and my heart actually skipped a beat.

"Well," she said softly, "There *is* something else…and I don't want to hurt Eli's feelings…"

Fuck.

"Go on," I prodded, my voice tight.

"Well…*you* know," she said, giving me a look like I should be totally clued in as to what the 'something else' was. "He kind of snores…loudly," she finished in an almost whisper.

I felt a smile touch my mouth, my insides now unclenched because Eli's snoring was her only issue.

"You mean it doesn't keep *you* awake?" she asked, her eyebrows quirking in the fucking sexy way that they did whenever she was confused or puzzled about something.

I sat down beside her on the bed, my hand moving aside her wet locks so that my lips could graze her bare neck. I felt her shiver against me.

"No, babe," I whispered against her skin. "I guess I'm used to it. But you know there are things to help with that? I mean I like the idea of having you between us every night, but if you're not ready for that, I totally understand. It's your call."

She nuzzled against me, and I wrapped an arm around her shoulders, pulling her into my chest.

"I want to sleep with you guys, too," she said quietly. "But maybe not *every* night, if that's okay. I mean, sometimes a girl just likes her privacy, you know?"

"Sure, baby. I just need to know that after last night, you haven't had second thoughts. I know that all of this is something new for you. I want you to share your feelings with me, okay?"

I felt her nod against me. "I guess I'm just not sure about the rules. I mean, are there rules? Or do we just go with the flow?" she asked softly.

"How about we just go with whatever we're all comfortable with, okay?"

She pulled back to look up at me, her eyes held a questioning look that fucking wrapped around my soul because I somehow knew that the next words out of her beautiful mouth were going to totally break me.

"I have to be honest, Cain. I loved what happened last night. I loved the pleasure that both of you gave me— the attention, the words, and the feelings—all of it. And I gotta say that I think I might be falling just a little bit in love...with *both* of you," she confessed quietly, casting her eyes downward, a soft blush coloring her face.

"Hey baby," I crooned, my fingers lifting her chin back up so that her gaze met mine, "Don't ever be afraid or ashamed of your feelings. I love that you just said that to me, but I've already felt it, Paige. Many times. And it's all good, because I think that I know that I'm falling in love with you, too. And I'm betting Eli isn't far behind."

She laced her arms around my neck, and I lowered my face to hers. I found her mouth with mine, eager to explore her once again, and taste all of the sweetness that was Paige.

Our Paige.

But for right now?

My Paige.

I pulled the towel from her, and pushed her gently back down against the pillows on her bed.

"How do you feel about having right now just be about you and me?" I whispered against her neck, as my tongue traced patterns on her soft damp skin.

She shivered again, pressing her nakedness against me, and I could feel my cock straining against my boxers.

"I'd like that, Cain," she said, and I could feel her smile. "Better get a condom from the nightstand," she instructed, nodding to her right.

I obliged, mentally making a note for her to take the necessary steps for birth control so that our sex could be condom-free in the very near future.

I'd been with many women in my thirty-one years on this planet, and I'd done my share of threesomes for sure. But it was just like I'd told Paige when she first realized what I was about. This wasn't the beginning of some threesome marathon, or even the fancier word that carried a bit more class: ménage. This was totally something else.

And to be honest?

It scared the hell out of me.

But at this moment, I had more pleasant things to occupy my mind with than trying to piece together why it scared me. I would have to think about that...later.

Chapter 21

February 22nd

It was my birthday.

My 23rd birthday and though I hadn't reached the age yet where I looked upon birthdays as the most dreaded day of the year, I still wasn't up for all the fuss that my men were making about it.

Breakfast had been served in bed.

Their bed, as a matter of fact, where I'd been sandwiched in between their well-muscled bodies all night long.

It seemed as if my guys had some sort of a bet going amongst themselves as to which one of them would be the last one to give me the Big 'O' while I was still twenty-two.

Officially, I believe that Eli's tongue had won that honor smack dab on my clit, although I had tried to stifle my moans so that Cain's fingers would continue that magical thrumming of my G-Spot so expertly, in order to allow me to double my pleasure even though the clock had slipped to a couple of minutes past midnight.

"What was the actual hour and minute of your birth?" Eli had asked me, continuing his sweet assault on my clit.

I swear to God, these men could be as competitive in bed as Serena and Venus Williams were on the tennis court.

Finally, totally satiated and just plain fucking worn out, I had drifted to sleep, only to be awakened by the alarm at six a.m. to find the bed totally devoid of masculinity.

Several minutes later, in they came with a tray, bearing my birthday breakfast, card and wrapped gift, along with a single red rose in a crystal vase.

I was instructed that I had to eat my waffles, complete with strawberries and whipped cream, before I touched the card and gift.

I gobbled my food down like a pig, as you can well imagine.

The card was sentimental, not comedic, so I knew immediately that Cain had selected it, and he had done very well in picking out the perfect card. The front of it read, "Happy Birthday To The One We Love."

I felt my face flush as I read the loving and poetic words printed inside, and saw both of their signatures scrawled at the bottom, with "I Love You," written twice.

My eyes brimmed a little bit, and Cain immediately cleared his throat and ordered me to open my present.

The box was small, so I knew that it was jewelry of some sort, but I swear to God, the tears re-surfaced again when I opened the small, black velvet box and removed the beautiful gold necklace that had three encased birthstones dangling from it.

My stone, amethyst, was in the center and the largest of the three stones. Eli's stone, aquamarine for March was to the right; Cain's emerald for May was to the left.

"It's gorgeous," I breathed, carefully removing it from the velvet lined box. "Thank you so much. I love it."

Eli helped me get it fastened, and I fingered it gently, loving that the stones were close to my heart.

"And don't forget," Eli spoke up, once he had fastened the clasp and dropped my hair back down, "We're taking you out for dinner this evening, so don't dawdle getting home from the base, got it?"

"Yes sirs," I said, smiling up at them. They both leaned in, planting soft kisses on my cheeks.

"I love you guys," I said softly.

∞∞∞∞∞∞∞∞∞∞∞∞∞∞∞∞∞∞∞∞∞∞∞∞∞∞∞∞∞

Work was the usual. I did think it odd that Darin made it a point to come by my station and wish me a Happy Birthday. I doubted very much if he would've even remembered when my birthday was had it not been for the February calendar on the bulletin board that marked birthdays for the staff in our department.

"Big plans for the birthday girl?" he asked, giving me a sexy wink.

"Naw," I said, not looking away from my computer screen. "Dinner out with the roomies. They insisted."

"Did they now?" he asked, quirking a brow, and getting a bit of a devilish grin going.

Really dude?

What's up with that look?

"Is there something you want to say, Darin?" I asked, giving him a slight glare.

"Just wanted to wish you the best on this special day," he said, walking away. "You've been looking great, by the way."

I contemplated his curious behavior. I mean, I was so over all of the bullshit that I'd encountered with him, having chalked it up to "That's life" and gone on my way, hardly giving it much thought anymore. I certainly didn't confide in him—or anyone for that matter—about my relationship with Cain and Eli. I wasn't the chatty type about my personal life; I never had been.

It dawned on me that Darin, with his "you're looking great" compliment just might be trying to rekindle something with me, and if that were the case, he was definitely barking up the wrong tree.

These past couple of months with my guys had been an experience for me, and not one that I'd likely ever want to part with.

I mean sure, there had been feelings within me that were confusing at times; little pangs of jealousy on the nights that I had opted to sleep in my own room (mainly to get a good night's rest due to Eli's snoring) when I'd hear the familiar headboard banging against the wall.

I had realized that they were going on without me, and yes, I had felt a bit jealous and insecure about that, I'll admit.

But then I had thought it through, and had realized that if I'd gotten up and went into their room, they would've immediately welcomed me into their bed, and made love to me so hard that it would've taken my breath away, as always. So, I had reminded myself that it had been my choice, and not theirs, to sit this one out.

The only other aspect of it that still bothered me a bit was the fact that I knew I was head over heels in love with Cain. You see, I lay awake one night and totally dissected the dynamics of my relationship with these men.

And here's what it boiled down to: we were all in love with one another and the depth of each person's love couldn't possibly be measured. I might've been a bit *more* in love with Cain; Eli might've been a bit *more* in love with Cain, but I was fairly certain that Cain was in love *equally*. And maybe that's exactly what was needed to make this all work out.

But what about long term? How could this possibly work out long term if it continued being kind of lopsided like that, I had wondered?

And even if it did work out well, what then? I had to think about my future, and I guess on one's birthday, there was a tendency to do just that.

I mean, somewhere in my future I knew that I wanted children. Marriage wasn't mandatory for that to happen, so at least that wasn't an issue.

I felt my eyes roll with my thoughts. Here I was, presuming things that I had no right to presume only two months into this...relationship.

My thoughts and reflections were interrupted when my cell vibrated on my desk. It was Trace.

"Hey," I greeted him.

"Happy Birthday, lil' sis," he replied, very cheerfully.

"Thanks," I replied, smiling into the phone.

This was the first we'd spoken since New Year's Day when I had groveled. I had called him back that evening and told him to never mind, that I was staying put for now. Blessedly, he hadn't asked for any detail. He'd probably just been relieved that I wasn't moving in. Things were still a bit uncomfortable. I had decided that the next move would have to be my brother's, and I was glad that he'd made the move.

"So, do you have plans for dinner tonight? Lindsey and I would love to take you out if you haven't made other plans. I probably should have called sooner, I know."

I was silent for a moment, not quite sure how I should respond. "Well, Eli and Cain planned on taking me out to dinner tonight for my birthday."

"Hmm," he responded, "How about if Lindsey and I join the three of you?"

Shit.

"I'm not sure what restaurant they had in mind," I replied slowly, "But I guess I could find out and give you a call back?"

It came out as a question which is so not how I wanted it to sound. Like I didn't want anyone else invading my inner sanctum with these men.

Luckily, Trace hadn't noticed. "Great—call either me or Lindsey with the time and place. We have a gift for you, and well, it's been a while since we've seen you, you know? I think we need to mend fences, Paige. I know that I want to and I hope that you do as well."

"I do, Trace," I replied. "I just felt like maybe you guys wanted to put me out of your lives...forever."

"You're family," he sighed. "You're stuck with us, and we're stuck with you because that's what being a family means, got it?"

I nodded and squeaked out a "yes."

∞∞∞∞∞∞∞∞∞∞∞∞∞∞∞∞∞∞∞∞∞∞∞∞∞∞∞∞∞∞∞∞∞∞

It was easier to reach Eli than Cain during working hours, especially around lunch time. I finished my now-cold cup of hot chocolate that I'd bought from the vending machine earlier. That was going to me my lunch after that huge breakfast I'd inhaled.

Eli's office phone rang several times before he picked up.

"Chambers," he answered, using his brusque workplace voice.

"It's me," I said, looking around to see how much privacy I had in my cubicle. Eli had an office, so there were no worries there.

"Hey babe," he greeted, his voice softening. "How's your birthday going?"

"Good so far," I sighed, feeling my belly tingle like it did whenever either one of them used some form of endearment when speaking to me. "But I did get a phone call from Trace."

I explained the conversation to him. Eli had no issue whatsoever with Trace and Lindsey joining us, in fact, he offered to phone Darcy to see if she and Easton wanted to join us as well.

"You don't have to go to all that trouble," I argued. "I don't want everyone making a big deal of my birthday and feeling, well...obligated or anything."

"Hey, no trouble at all, babe," he laughed. "Besides that, with Easton there, we're pretty much guaranteed that he'll pick up the tab."

"Eli, you're so bad," I giggled, swiveling my chair around so that I could toss my empty paper cup into the trash can.

"I know, babe, but you wouldn't have it any other way, would you?"

I felt my cheeks flush as I recalled the delicious, "bad" things he'd done to me last night in our 'family' bed as we had started calling it.

"Would you?" he pressed softly.

"No, Eli. I wouldn't have it any other way," I confirmed.

"Okay, so I'll make the arrangements with Darce, and I'll give Lindsey a holler, so that we're all on the same page for our Paige tonight at La Chaumiere."

"Now *that* was cheesy," I giggled. "But I love you anyway, especially since we're eating at La Chaumiere."

"Love you," he said. "See you at home later."

"Bye," I said softly into the phone, as I swiveled back around in my chair.

My smile froze when I saw Darin Murphy standing no more than three feet from me, in my cubicle, with a look on his face that told me he'd heard everything. He was just trying to digest it in his own mind.

Men like Darin weren't used to dumping a chick and not having them heartbroken (like Darcy was) about it. At the very least, I'm sure he took offense to the fact that I

173

didn't at least stalk him a bit afterwards; or try to find out who his latest conquest was at the academy. That just wasn't me.

Well…not anymore.

"Excuse me?" I said, clearly irritated that he hadn't made his presence known.

He quirked a brow at me, his eyes narrowing infinitesimally as he spoke. "That explains it all," he said, his lips forming a stiff smile.

"I beg your pardon?" I asked, feeling my blood pressure shooting up at his total disregard for my privacy.

He shook his head, his hand rubbing the back of his neck as if he were feeling some sort of strain. "The way you've been acting the last couple of months; all happy and bubbly—and not giving any of the dudes here a second glance. Several of us have noticed the subtle but definite change in your demeanor, hell—you're in love with your roomie, aren't you?"

I immediately tensed up.

"That's really none of your business, Agent Murphy," I snapped, trying my best to give him an arctic glare.

"Well, answer me this, Paige. Does the other fag know his dude is bi? And that Eli's a cheater to boot? I could've sworn Darcy said Eli was gay." He scratched his head in faux confusion.

"It's none of your damn business what goes on in *our* house or in *my* life. I'll thank you to keep your nose out of places it clearly doesn't belong."

Oh, I was pissed. That much was obvious and, if I had given a damn at the moment, I might've re-thought those words that had just been spoken.

By me.

"*Our* house?" he said, echoing the words I'd just put out there in anger. "Fuck me," he laughed, "You're banging *both* of them, aren't you?"

"You're out of line, Darin," I deadpanned, trying to keep my cool before I let anything else out of the bag in anger. "What did you need? Why are you here?"

He turned around and looked at me, and I could tell he now was feeling kind of...stupid. "I was going to see if you wanted to get dinner—you know, for your birthday. Sounds like you have other plans."

He turned and left my cubicle before I had the opportunity to tell him that having dinner with him—ever, wasn't going to happen.

I put my head in my hands, wondering just how long it would take for Darin to spread some vicious gossip about me around to the rest of the office staff.

And then I remembered: it's only gossip if it's not true.

Still, I couldn't think that anyone I worked with would have the nerve or the audacity to ask me straight-out about my private and personal life.

Darin had no class.

I was betting the rest of my colleagues did.

Chapter 22

    I snuck out of work an hour early, wanting nothing more than to put this day behind me. Darin's innuendos had unnerved me. I didn't need him stirring up any drama, especially since my internship was ending next month, and I had applied for a permanent position with the bureau.

    I beat both Eli and Cain home, going to my room to take a shower and change into something suitable for La Chaumiere. If I even had anything suitable, that is.

    I saw that two wrapped boxes had been placed on my bed. More gifts? One dress-sized box, the other one small.

    My guys…damn.

    I knew I should probably have waited until they got home, but shit, you knew that wasn't going to happen.

    I tore into the big box immediately, taking off the lid, and separating the tissue paper.

    Oh. My God.

    It was the most beautiful black dinner dress that I'd ever laid my eyes on. It was simple, but chic in the way it was cut. It had a sweetheart neckline with long sleeves that tapered at the wrist. It was perfect for La Chaumiere. I looked at the designer tag and saw that it was Donna Karan.

    My Eli.

The other box contained a pair of earrings that matched the birthstone encrusted necklace they had bought for me. My birthstone was on the post, and each of their birthstones dangled daintily on a tiny gold chain from it. There was a note in the box.

"These will look great with the necklace."

∞∞∞∞∞∞∞∞∞∞∞∞∞∞∞∞∞∞∞∞∞∞∞∞∞∞∞∞∞∞∞∞∞

Lindsey, Trace, Darcy and Easton were already at La Chaumiere when our threesome arrived. I felt nervous for some reason, and by the time our entrees were served, I was pretty damn sure that Darcy had finished analyzing me under her mental microscope.

"I love your necklace," she commented, glancing over at my birthday gift, "And the matching earrings," she finished, her eyes skimming over them.

I fumbled with an earring, and felt my face flush under everyone's perusal.

"Thank you," I said. "Birthday gift from my roomies," I smiled, doing my best to avoid looking at Eli who was sitting across from me. I felt Cain's hand move over to cover mine in my lap. He gave it a squeeze.

"Well, they certainly spoil you; that's for sure," Lindsey piped up, taking a sip of her white wine. "How about a birthday toast?"

Trace cleared his throat.

"If I may?" he said, raising his glass of wine. "To our little sister on her birthday—in hopes that this will be the best one yet, and wishes for many more to come. And also to welcome Paige Matthews as the newest member of the F.B.I. family."

"What?" I gasped, my eyes immediately widened in surprise.

Trace and Lindsey's smiles were panoramic, and contagious, it seemed, as everyone else at our table smiled as if it were no surprise that my application for permanent employment with the F.B.I. had been accepted.

"You were going to find out tomorrow anyway," Trace said. "I just pulled rank a little bit to get the information to make your birthday that much sweeter," he finished, giving me a brotherly wink.

All eyes were on me and, for some reason, I was simply speechless. I mean, I thought I'd had a fairly good chance, but in all honesty, I just wasn't one to believe in myself all that much.

"You seem surprised, babe," Cain said quietly, his gaze penetrating me.

"I just don't know what to say," I said, a smile finally breaking through.

"Well I do," Trace said. "Good job, Paige. You worked your ass off and I, for one, am proud as hell of you."

"Hear, hear," Eli chimed in, beaming.

"Congratulations and cheers," Easton said, as we all held up our wine glasses to tap with one another's—well, except for Darcy who was obviously not imbibing since she was pregnant.

"Thank you all," I said, suddenly feeling shy at the amount of attention on me, and seriously not accustomed to it. "This is totally awesome." I took a long sip of wine, and the warmth spread throughout me; my brother's words echoed over and over in my mind. I never would've guessed just how much hearing Trace tell me that he was proud of me would make me feel. I felt an unfamiliar bit of self-pride and damn it felt good.

I was grateful as hell when Easton started conversing with Eli and Darcy started talking to Lindsey about the new nursery for the baby. I could feel Cain's hand move from mine, and gently rub my nylon-clad thigh beneath my new dress. Immediately, my face warmed with a flush, and I felt that familiar tingle in my belly.

I took another sip of my wine, looking over his way, but he had started conversing with Trace. Although I knew where his focus really was at the moment: between my freakin' legs.

I crossed my legs and squirmed a bit, however that did nothing to dissuade his talented fingers from finding my mound, his thumb now rubbing against my slit from outside my clothing.

Sweet Baby Jesus!

"Umm, excuse me," I said, "I've got to make a visit to the Little Girl's Room," I lied. If I continued allowing him to do what he was intent upon doing, it would only be a matter of minutes before I'd be moaning my release.

"I'll go with you," Darcy piped up, scooting her chair back. "These last couple of months are hell on the old bladder."

"Hurry back," Cain said with a slight twitch of his lips, as he looked over at me.

The door to the large powder room had barely closed behind Darcy and me when she spoke.

"Hold up, Paige," she said from behind, causing me to halt in my tracks.

Oh…dayumm.

I turned around to face her, and the accusatory expression on her face didn't go unnoticed.

"Can we sit for a minute?" she asked, nodding toward the intricately carved, plum velvet settee against the mirrored wall of the powder room.

"Sure," I shrugged, my pulse speeding up a bit because this could mean only one thing: Eli had shared the details of our relationship with her.

How stupid was it that it hadn't even crossed my mind to ask him after all these weeks?

"Paige, you must know how important Eli is to me, right?"

I nodded silently.

"Then, please don't think it's none of my business, because when it comes to protecting him, there are no boundaries for me. Are you fucking Cain behind Eli's back?"

Holy shit.

"Wh-what?" I stammered, momentarily taken aback by the conclusion she'd jumped to. "Why would you ask me that?" It was my turn to put some edge in my voice.

She leaned back against the cushion on the settee, one hand rubbing her baby bump in a circular motion, as if that had some sort of calming effect on her.

"The chemistry going back and forth between the two of you is kind of…well, *obvious*. And let's just say I've been around long enough to know when a dude's feeling you up under the table," she finished, her eyes directly on mine.

Busted.

"It's not what you think, Darcy," I replied, feeling a sigh escape through my whole body. I hated that I felt compelled to be so secretive about my feelings for these men. It wasn't that I was ashamed of it; it was just that I wasn't ready for the negative reactions, disapproving comments and judgy attitudes that I knew would be forthcoming.

"Then what is it?" she asked pointedly.

I fingered my new necklace nervously, trying to decide whether I should tell her, and wondering if I did, could I trust her not to broadcast it? Her eyes were now on my necklace, watching as my finger rubbed each stone in it.

"Wait a minute," she said slowly, "That's a custom necklace, isn't it?"

She didn't wait for me to respond. "That's your birthstone in the center. And the aquamarine—that's Eli's birthstone for March. What month was Cain born?" she asked, her eyes narrowing just a bit.

"May," I replied, knowing that if anyone knew the birthstone for each month of the year, it would be Darcy.

"Emerald," she said quietly. "Oh my God."

I looked over at her and hesitated only for a moment. "Please don't say anything to Lindsey or Easton. I'm not sure if we're ready to go public with our relationship just yet."

"Oh my God," she repeated, shaking her head back and forth. "How did I *not* see this?"

I didn't answer because it was obviously a question she was posing to herself.

"I mean, I still talk to Eli on the phone at least once or twice a week and he has said *nothing*. I mean Christ almighty—it never *occurred* to me that he'd cross back over."

Huh?

"What?" I asked, not sure what she meant by that.

"Oh...sorry," she said, with a slight smile. "Eli told me a while back about that brief, albeit disastrous marriage of his. He said because of it, he'd made the decision to pursue only those of his own gender. That it was safer for his heart that way. Wow—what the hell did you do to my brotha from anotha?"

I felt myself smile in relief. Darcy was okay with it and it helped that someone I knew wasn't going to give me shit about it.

"Darcy, please," I said, putting just a hint of pleading into my voice to grab her attention. "Can you please keep this to yourself until...well, until further notice?"

"No worries," she replied, nodding. "Your secret's safe with me. But hey, is it okay if I give Eli shit about keeping it from me?"

I giggled softly. "As long as Easton, Trace or Lindsey are nowhere around when you do. I'm in a nice place with my brothers at the moment, and I don't know— I guess I kind of like that."

"Deal," she replied, "But I think maybe you're not giving them enough credit here. It is your life and your business after all."

I nodded.

"By the way," I said, wanting to change the subject, "I see you're gestating very nicely. When's the baby due? All Eli says when I ask is that it's April or May."

"He's such a bonehead, isn't he?" she teased. "We're expecting our baby girl, Carson, around the twenty-seventh of April. Eli always says that if she takes after me, she won't arrive until early May."

I laughed because that is exactly the type of thing Eli would say about Darcy.

Still, I knew that he loved her, but not the same way that he loved me, so I was more than fine with it. Those two actually did seem like brother and sister in many ways. More so than Trace and me, it would seem. But that was something I hoped to change, now that I would be residing in D.C. permanently.

"I love the name you picked out for her," I said wistfully. "Carson Matthews is an awesome name for a girl."

"Or a boy, as Easton has so eloquently reminded me once or a hundred times. Geez, sometimes I think Lindsey's right."

"About what?"

"Your oldest brother can be quite stuffy, Paige," she replied, trying her best to use a British accent, but kind of failing at it.

Darcy and I returned to our table, and I didn't miss the looks of concern that passed between Eli and Cain. My guys were instinctual and kind of protective that way. I gave them both a smile and a nod, letting them know that everything was cool—for now.

Through the rest of dinner, we were entertained with some of Darcy's exaggerated "Eli" stories from when they were roommates, along with some hilarious tales about a cruise they had all gone on together over a year ago. Darcy referred to it as "The 12 Days of Vacay," and Easton referred to it as 'yet another one of Darcy's brilliant ideas gone sour,' for which I'm pretty sure he received a swift kick to the shin underneath the table.

True to Eli's prediction, Easton insisted on picking up the tab for everyone's dinner as his birthday present to me. Darcy slipped me a card, which I was fairly certain contained a generous check.

Once everyone had finished and was preparing to leave, Eli said he'd go outside to have the valet bring our car around. Lindsey was talking to Darcy, and I watched as Trace made his way over to me.

"Can we talk in private for a moment, Paige?" he asked, his eyes giving away nothing.

"Sure," I replied, quietly, not sure of his intent.

Cain approached, holding my coat open for me. I immediately put my arms through the sleeves, as he lifted my hair out from underneath the collar, brushing it back from my face, his eyes meeting mine.

"Trace needs to speak to me for a minute, Cain. I'll see you outside?" I posed it as a question.

He nodded, eyeing Trace through shuttered eyes, but it wasn't extremely obvious—or maybe it was, but my brother seemed unaffected nonetheless.

186

Once out on the sidewalk, I pulled my collar up a bit to keep the windy chill of the night off of my neck.

"Paige," Trace started, actually appearing to be unsure of what he wanted to say. "I meant what I said earlier to you. I'm really fucking proud of you and how you've really grown over this past year."

"Okkaay," I said quirking a brow. "So, why do I think that's not why we're out here?"

He ran a hand through his thick, brown hair and looked me dead-ass in the eye. "I had a call from Darin Murphy this evening," he said. "What the hell are you doing?"

I immediately felt defensive. Fuck Darin Murphy! And the fact that Trace would have even listened to him was kind of pissing me off.

"This is *my* business, Trace," I said simply. "It's not on display, it's not up for debate, and I don't have to explain myself to anyone—not to you, not to Mom or Dad. This is my life and, for once, I'm fucking happy."

"Hey," he said, his voice softening. "I'm not here to judge you sweetie. Christ, I'm no saint and I've got a past. I just want to make sure—I need to know—that this isn't something you've been pressured into, you know?"

"How could you even think *that*?" I snapped. "What? Paige is *so* impulsive or Paige is trying to get attention just like she always does so it must be what? *Fake?* Well, I'm here to tell you, Trace, that this is *real.* It's actually the first *real* relationship that I've ever had."

"No need to get upset, sweetie. I just needed to ask, because well—I love you, sis. I know that it might not seem that way, but I do. I will always be here for you and I just needed to know that you're okay and I can see that you're different. Hell, who am I to question your choices? I've known Eli for awhile; I don't know Cain as well, but as long as you're happy and they're good to you—that's all I care about."

I felt a heavy load lift from my shoulders after he said that. One down—strike that—two down, and a helluva lot more to go, but I knew having Trace in my corner was a big win.

I felt my eyes tear up immediately because I knew that Taz truly loved and cared about me. Yes, I was officially going to call him Taz now because it just seemed so right, and because that's what everyone else called him.

Until now, he had seemed too uptight to be a "Taz." But now he wasn't. He was my big brother and I knew that he loved me unconditionally.

I stood on my tip-toes, throwing my arms around him for a hug. "Thank you, Taz," I whispered against him. "Thank you so much for that."

"You know that I can't make promises where Mom and Dad are concerned, Paige. That's up to you to tell them about…your relationship whenever you choose. They'll not hear it from me."

I nodded, sniffling a bit as I wiped an errant tear from my cheek.

"Is everything okay, Paige?" It was Cain and he was now standing next to us, his voice filled with concern, and his dark eyes getting darker as he tried to assess the situation.

"It's all good, Maddox," Taz said, releasing me. "Just wishing my sister a happy birthday. And I wanted to give her this."

Taz reached into his jacket pocket and pulled out an envelope.

"You know I'm not much of a shopper, Paige. But I know how much you've learned to enjoy working out, so I got you a membership of your own at Lifetime Fitness. That way you never have to put up with that ass-hat Murphy showing up during your workouts."

"Thanks, Taz," I said with a smile, giving him a kiss on his cheek.

Eli pulled up in his car, honking his horn.

"Take care of her Maddox," Taz said gruffly, "Or you'll have me to face."

Cain remained solemn, but I could see the corners of his mouth twitching, so I breathed a sigh of relief, knowing that he totally understood where my big brother was coming from.

"No worries, Taz. We will. Paige is very important to the both of us."

And with that, Taz was off.

Cain helped me into the car. "You okay, babe?"

"I'm totally fine. But you know what? There was no birthday cake today. No candles for me to blow out with my birthday wish."

"We can take care of that, right Eli?"

"Consider it done," Eli said, pulling away from the curb.

∞∞∞∞∞∞∞∞∞∞∞∞∞∞∞∞∞∞∞∞∞∞∞∞∞∞∞∞∞∞∞

Later that evening, when we were all stretched out on top of our bed, Cain and I shared with Eli the conversation that I'd had with Taz. I then shared the conversation that I'd had with Darcy, which was pretty much a moot point now, since Darin Murphy had seen to it that my brother had been clued in.

"There's still the matter of your parents," Eli pointed out. "And I'm sure there will be scores of others that want to put their fucking two cents in."

"I know," I replied, not wanting to feel any melancholy at the moment. I just wanted to finish my birthday out with the traditional birthday wish.

Cain had stuck a candle in the fancy cupcake that we'd stopped to buy at a bakery on our way home to represent my official birthday cake.

"I don't understand, guys," I said. "Is this something that we're *supposed* to be ashamed of? Because, if it is, I have to tell you that I'm not. But, at the same time, I just don't want the grief that I know I'll get from my parents. I feel like such a freakin' hypocrite about it. I guess I've grown comfortable in this private little cocoon that we've created here for ourselves. I don't want it spoiled by any ugliness."

"Hey," Cain said, turning on his other side to face me. "We'll figure it out, sweetie. We've got plenty of time to figure it all out, okay?"

I nodded, biting my lower lip and wondering about that. Maybe he was right. Maybe it *was* simply a matter of time before everything came together and people accepted what we were about.

"Because," Eli piped up, "We *are* all in this together—for the long haul, right?"

"Right," Cain and I answered together.

"I feel so lucky," I sighed, plucking at the comforter. "A year ago, I never would've guessed how happy I'd be right now. Right here."

"Tell us what makes you feel so lucky," Cain challenged softly, as he flicked a match and lit the candle on the cupcake.

"Well, I have an awesome new career as a forensic technician with the F.B.I," I started. "And then there are *these men* you see—two of them that I love so fucking hard. They make me so happy and they love me right back and it's seriously the best feeling in the world for me. And for now, I have my brother's approval, which isn't easily given, mind you—at least to me, and it kind of rocks. My life is damn near perfect I guess."

"What would make it perfect?" Cain whispered, leaning over me so that his lips grazed my jawline with slow, soft kisses.

"Yes," Eli chimed in quietly, his fingertips tracing a trail along my cheek, his warm breath caressing my ear as I felt his tongue lightly trace the outer edge.

I shivered with anticipation because I knew that these men were going to make love to me tonight.

And it would be slow, and it would be sensual, and it would be so very sweet. And for whatever reason, I knew that it would be different with them tonight.

Because more than anything else going on in my life, there was one thing that I was sure of: I had the love of these men, and it was more precious to me than any other gift I had received…ever!

I reflected on how Darcy had looked tonight. She was glowing and happy and I loved when she let everyone feel her tummy when Carson kicked during dinner. I had been totally mesmerized by it.

"A baby," I finally sighed. "Having our baby would make it perfect. It's what I want."

I sat up for a moment and leaned back on my elbows. "So, it's official—for my next birthday, my wish is to have a baby in my belly."

I leaned over and blew out the single candle on my cupcake, and as I watched the smoke curl and snake its way up to the ceiling, I smiled.

The End

About the Author

Andrea Smith is an Amazon Best-Selling author of the G-Man Series. This series can be read as stand-alone, although it is more enjoyable to read the books in order:

Diamond Girl

Love Plus One

Night Moves

G-Men Holiday Wrap

'*These Men*' is a spin-off story, taken from characters first appearing in '*Night Moves*' and '*G-Men Holiday Wrap.*'

Ms. Smith's legacy series, the Baby Series, consists of:

1) Maybe Baby

2) Baby Love

3) Be My Baby

3.5) Baby Come Back

This series should be read in sequence and is a contemporary romance suspense series with an erotic tone.

Please follow this author on Facebook:

https://www.facebook.com/AndreaSmithAuthor

Amazon:

http://tinyurl.com/nbczyvk

Goodreads:

http://tinyurl.com/pduqmu2

Links to Andrea Smith's Books:

Maybe Baby (Book #1 - Baby Series)

Amazon: http://tinyurl.com/nfjm8v6

B & N: http://tinyurl.com/lknz2eq

Baby Love (Book #2 - Baby Series)

Amazon: http://tinyurl.com/ndwvh8x

B & N: http://tinyurl.com/pxefmc4

Be My Baby (Book #3 - Baby Series)

Amazon: http://tinyurl.com/pyxahof

B & N: http://tinyurl.com/ocktr93

Baby Come Back (Book #3.5 - Baby Series)

Amazon: http://tinyurl.com/pdhtknt

B & N: http://tinyurl.com/n9b5bbm

Diamond Girl (Book #1 - G-Man Series)

Amazon: http://tinyurl.com/nlhkt59

B & N: http://tinyurl.com/o2nxfpn

Love Plus One (Book #2 - G-Man Series)

Amazon: http://tinyurl.com/oc9fbxl

B & N: http://tinyurl.com/opx3a4e

Night Moves (Book #3 - G-Man Series)

Amazon: http://tinyurl.com/objl5mm

B & N: http://tinyurl.com/mk5zdjb

G-Men Holiday Wrap (Book #3.5 - G-Man Series)

Amazon: http://tinyurl.com/omkyd84

B & N: http://tinyurl.com/lzazz5z